PROLOGUE

SOMETIME CLOSE TO MIDNIGHT on Christmas Eve,
1974, cyclone Tracy tore into Australia's top end.
Seventy per cent of the homes of Darwin's forty-seven-
thousand inhabitants were literally blown off their
foundations and the debris scattered over kilometres.
Hundreds more kilometres of coastline were also
hammered and wind gusts reportedly reached up to
speeds of three hundred kilometres per hour.

It is a matter of record that seventy one people died
during Tracy's merciless onslaught and hundreds more
were injured. There were rumours that not all of the
deaths were related to her fury and the violence of the
cyclone was mirrored by the violent nature of man.

[?]

CHAPTER 1

GRAMPIAN NATIONAL PARK, VICTORIA, 1974.

The cockatoo glides high above the glistening river snaking through the craggy mountains and lush landscape of the national park. It spears downward and follows the long bitumen road cutting like a scar into the native bushland of the Grampians. The heat haze shimmering in the distances distorts shapes, making them bend and twist.

The cockatoo closes the distance, and the illusion becomes the reality – a small army of police riot vehicles. The local TV station's mobile news truck is parked off the road and the crew are racing to cover the action. More than a hundred riot police, some on horseback, form into lines.

The bird's sense of danger has been honed over many years of being hunted by ground predators and shot at by farmers. He regains height with a few strong wingbeats and banks away to find safer feeding grounds.

Beyond the police is the park access, where half a dozen Indigenous men and women are chained to the rusted metal gate. Behind them is a makeshift campsite with another fifty Indigenous people.

A handful of stringy dogs scamper, agitated, through the camp. Hand-painted signs are tacked up on the trees:

5000 YEARS, NOT 170!

LANDOWNERS, NOT LESSEES!

Senior Constable Derek Walker watches an elderly Indigenous man motioning to his people to remain calm and stand their ground. He performs final checks on his riot gear. His eyes lock onto the Indigenous man and a thin smile pushes up the corners of his mouth. He has no real bias against these people, and he couldn't give a shit if they were black, white or green, for that matter. In his twenty years on the job, he's learnt one key thing about himself, the one thing that motivates him to put on the uniform day after day. He enjoys inflicting pain.

He draws his baton from his belt and his knuckles whiten with the force of the grip. The rest of the riders remove their batons and hold them at the ready. Flies swarm into the air and an eerie stillness falls; the calm before the storm.

The police horses snort and rear in anticipation. Hooves stomp the ground and dust explodes into the air. The police commander slowly raises a whistle to his lips and blows a short, shrill blast. The lines of foot and mounted police slowly move forward in practiced formation.

The Indigenous protestors form up behind their people chained to the gate. Two of the camp dogs jump the fence and streak towards the horses, which rear up. One reaches the horses, snapping at the forelocks of Walker's mount.

Walker kicks the horse's flanks. It rears, hooves slashing the air, and stomps the dog to death. The whistle sounds again, and the mounted police break into a thunderous headlong gallop.

The Indigenous protesters huddle together defiantly as the wall of mounted police quickly closes on them. The mounted riders reach the protesters, jump the fence, and ride into the middle of the group. They break ranks and scatter in every direction.

A half-dozen police, carrying bolt-cutters, rush the protestors chained to the gate. They sever the chain links, then handcuff and drag the protestors to the waiting paddy-wagons. More police scramble over the gate, wading into the protestors, their batons cracking against skulls. No quarter is given to man, woman, or child in a swift and merciless exercise in brutality.

Walker charges towards Roy with a thin-lipped, savage smile and deadly intent. His grip tightens on the baton and he raises it above his head. Two Indigenous youths, David and Jacob Marjina, realizing Walker's intent, sprint to intercept him.

Roy remains eerily calm and his gaze turns unflinchingly towards the oncoming rider.

There's a murderous glint in Walker's eyes. The dog had been the entree, but this was the meat for him. Time seems to slow, the distance closes, and Roy still holds his ground.

At the last possible moment, David and Jacob leap onto the horse and rider, taking them to the ground. The horse twists at an odd angle and its leg breaks with a sickening snap. Walker is pinned beneath his mount as it thrashes in agony. His pelvis breaks under the crushing weight.

David and Jacob lead the old man through the chaos towards safety, but they don't get far as more riot police encircle them. They are slammed to the ground, beaten, and cuffed. The screams and pleading of Roy's people fill the air, but it is Walker's horse that becomes his focal point.

Two officers race to Walker's aid; one grabs the bridle and steadies the frenzied animal while the other drags Walker, screaming in pain, from beneath it. A ranking police officer joins them, makes a quick judgment call based on the horse's injuries, and draws his service revolver.

The horse has nothing left and its head flops to the ground. Its dark, soulful eyes find Roy's seeming to beg forgiveness, a thing he gives without reservation.

The hammer of the service revolver falls on the primer, firing the projectile, and ending the horse's life. Roy sees the light fade from its eyes and his brim with tears that spill down his cheeks and fall to the dust.
⁇

CHAPTER 2

"THE LAW OF THE LAND" Gray Garrett fires the line like a bullet straight at the defence council. "A law that governs all Australians" He deliberately turns to include the jury and continues "Regardless of race, colour, or creed".

Gray casually moves towards the jury to draw them in and create a sense of intimacy. "A law that allows all in this country to be heard. A law that gives us the right to demonstrate, peacefully. But as you have heard, this was not peaceful. As you have seen, an officer of the law was seriously injured during the course of his duties. His horse was so badly injured that it had to be euthanized where it lay".

He motions to the defence table where Roy, David and Jacob sit alongside their legal-aid lawyer. "Now, my learned colleague would have you believe that events simply got out of hand after the police officer 'allegedly' used excessive force against his clients, but you know that we have proven this not to be the case – no, not to be the truth. They would have you believe this was simply a case of historical land rights. Again, not the truth. The truth is that this was an illegal occupation of Crown land. The truth is that for weeks, weapons had been raised against ordinary Australians simply wanting to exercise their right to enter the park".

Roy catches the eye of the judge, stands, and speaks in his own tongue. "We don't own the land; the land owns us."

The judge hammers the gavel repeatedly. "Order! Order in the court!"

Jacob respectfully takes Roy by the arm. "It's no use, Grandfather, these people only understand white words" Roy hesitates for a moment before retaking his seat and looks the judge in the eye. Surely a man in his position, of his years, would be able to understand, but the look he gets in return is devoid f such understanding.

The judge takes Roy's words and gesture as one of insolence "Would Council kindly restrain the defendants from any further outbursts," he orders the defence lawyer.

The defence lawyer turns to admonish his clients but they have already retaken their seats and are sitting in silence.

Every seat in the gallery is full; mostly Europeans plus a smattering of Indigenous faces. One white face belongs to Lange Garrett, a studious-looking older man, who watches Gray intently. In his eyes there is simmering anger tinged with deep sadness.

Gray continues, "Roy Anapinja, David Marjina and Jacob Marjina used violence to make their point, that is the truth." Gray paces slowly along the front of the jury box looking into the eyes of each and every juror as he speaks "I believe that it is our responsibility to send the strongest possible message to the Indigenous community that this kind of behaviour cannot, will not, be tolerated. I would ask you, the jury, to reach the only reasonable verdict." He pauses for effect. "Guilty on all charges".

Gray returns to the prosecution table, where his co-council is in conversation with a well-dressed man sitting behind him in the gallery. He overhears their conversation: ... using one of their own – stroke of bloody genius. Both men cease talking when they realize Gray may be able to hear them.

"Well done, Gray. Nice summation" says his co-councillor, and shakes his hand. "Let's wait for a decision before we pat each other on the back" Gray adds cautiously. He glances back in time to see Lange stand and walk stiffly towards the exit and slam through the doors without so much as a backwards glance. "Shit. Shit. Shit," curses Gray quietly. The co-councillor shoots him a concerned look. "Are you okay?" Gray takes a deep breath before answering. "It's nothing I can't deal with".

The judge retires the jury, the court is cleared, and the constable of the court handcuff the prisoners.

Gray watches as Roy's cuffs are clicked firmly around his wrists and looks up to find his gaze upon him. There is no anger or recrimination in those eyes, just a weary deep sadness. All three prisoners are taken down and Gray is left with an uneasy feeling that he can't seem to shake.

CHAPTER 3

DARK NATIVE TIMBER AND RED LEATHER are the theme
throughout the lounge-room. The radio is on and 'The
Sound of Silence' drifts from the speakers. A few
tasteful paintings hang on the walls. An old, expensive,
Steinway piano fills one corner of the room, its surface
covered with framed family photos.

Gray quietly closes the front door behind him and
glances around for his father. This room, with its earthy
smells of wood, leather and brandy holds so many good
memories for him. He takes his time; it's been a while
since his last visit, and he wants to stall the inevitable
confrontation. The sound of Lange's voice, raised in
song, comes from the kitchen.

Gray quietly crosses the room to the piano and picks up
a photograph of himself as a little boy, with his mother,
a Yolngu woman. She looks painfully thin and drawn, a
grey pallor to her skin. They are on a windswept
Victorian beach with the imposing Three Sisters in the
background.

Gray's mind flashes back to that day and he remembers
her voice, so fragile – a whisper – the cancer had robbed
her of that too. She had asked him to be strong for his
father, because he was going to need him in the hard
days ahead.

"We all face this storm one day," she'd said, holding his face in her trembling hands. "Face it with dignity and don't be afraid."

Tears well in his eyes and he absently wipes them away. "Still, after all this time," he quietly says to himself. "I love you, Mum". The rest of the photographs are from fishing and hunting trips, school and university graduations, dressed for the ball with Robyn on his arm. Each picture denotes a passage of time through days that seemed, in retrospect, a whole lot easier than adulthood. He and Lange had been so much closer, back then. Lange had tried to teach him another way to live, to experience the world, but those things became lost in the whirlwind of high school, university, and then law school.

He had always felt uncomfortable being different, so he mastered the art of camouflage at an early age, and as he grew up his motto became "Go along to get along". No identity was better than the wrong identity.

Gray is snapped out of his reverie by the off key, but enthusiastic singing coming from the kitchen.
"Oi, are you butchering a cat in there?" he shouts.
He gets a loud snort of indignation in response, and a "You're late" quickly follows. Gray gently places the photograph back into its position and slouches into the kitchen.

Lange, an apron over his work clothes, transfers two sizzling steaks and eggs from the frying pan to the plates he's already set on the table. "Another couple of minutes and these would have been nicely cremated" he says.

"Lucky your cooking's better than your singing, or you'd starve" Gray replies, slumping on to his seat.

Gray is quick to tuck into his food. He's well into it when he notices that Lange hasn't even started. "Aren't you eating?" he asks. Lange pushes the plate aside. "Not much of an appetite". That's not the case with Gray, who demolishes the steak in record time and mops up the residue with a slice of bread saying "Well, I'm done. I couldn't fit another bite in" He leans back in his chair and undoes his belt a notch or two.

A long, uncomfortable moment of silence follows, and Gray is about to seize the moment to beat a hasty retreat and head for home. "Well..."

Lange jumps in over the top of him. "I could use a hand out in the garage".

Gray is quick to counter, "I should be going. Rob'll be wondering where I am".

Check.

"It won't take long," says Lange. "It's the ottoman I've been working on for Robyn".

Checkmate.

Lange picks up both plates and deposits them onto the kitchen bench. "Besides, she knows where you are" With that, he saunters out the back door, leaving Gray shaking his head. "You do know this is coercion, right?" he calls after him.

Shelves containing different sizes of lumber run up the garage wall to the ceiling. Gray picks one from the nearest stack without much thought.

Lange shakes his head "It's an ottoman, not a barn – the two by one, next shelf up".

Gray replaces the incorrect timber. "Rookie mistake, sorry." He takes one from the shelf above and passes it to Lange. The basic structure he's crafting is slowly taking shape, but it's still too early to tell exactly what it is.

Lange planes the top edge. "So, how did it feel?" he asks, without taking his eyes off the task at hand. Gray knew this was coming, but the old bugger let it drag out painfully long. "How did what feel?" Two can play at that game.

Lange stops planing and blows away the debris from the surface. "Winning".

Gray shrugs. Just another case. He watches Lange place the timber into the vice, carefully measures out the section he wants to cut, stand back from it, and measure again. Gray smiles at the process.

"What?" asks Lange.

"Measure twice, cut once," replies Gray, still smiling.

"So, some things you do take notice of." Quips, Lange.

The curt reply wipes the smile from Gray's face. Here we go.

Lange tosses the tape measure onto the bench and turns to give Gray his full undivided attention. "What happened in that courtroom today…"

Gray is having none of it. "You need to drop it" His tone cold.

"Was a whitewash" says Lange, undeterred. "The Indigenous people have a legal historical claim to that land and the Crown bloody well knows it".

Gray retorts, "Yes, but this case wasn't about land rights. Two separate issues".

Lange is becoming indignant. "They were charged by mounted police and they defended themselves".

"They wouldn't have had to defend themselves if they hadn't illegally occupied the park in the first place" Gray fires back.

"That depends upon your definition of illegal occupation".

Gray's reply is dripping with sarcasm. "I went by the current legal definition, not the emotional moral high-ground one. Anyway, it's a moot point. The jury found them guilty".

This is quickly turning into less of a family argument and more of a heated legal battle. Gray can see from Lange's reddening face that his frustration is building. They have been at odds over many issues over the years but this is the first time he's ever felt that his father was ashamed of his actions.

"They were blind-sided" Lange yells angrily.

Gray knows exactly where this is headed, but refrains from interrupting.

"A biased media, the only witnesses were the police, and then there's …" Lange mentally censors himself before it goes too far and there's no coming back.

Gray is quietly seething. "There's what..?"

Lange has painted himself into a corner. "Come on, Gray, you know how it looks – an Indigenous lawyer on the prosecution team against Indigenous defendants?" The elephant has been sat squarely in the room.

"So, the only reason you think I got this case is because I'm a bloody Abo?"

Lange glares at his use of the word "Abo" but doesn't back away one iota. "They were your people in that courtroom" he thunders. "Your bloody people".

Gray had his reservations about taking the case in the first place, but Lange had drummed into him that the client always comes first and you use every tool at your disposal to effect the right outcome for them. But the real reason was something deeper, darker, an anger he'd struggled with for as long as he could remember but could never quite put his finger on. His anger erupts and he doesn't step over the line – he leaps. "My people are the ones I'm paid to represent. You need to remember that and mind your own fucking business".

The sharp sound of the slap echoes through the kitchen before Lange even realizes that he has struck Gray. "By God, I'm only glad your mother isn't here to hear this" he says, his voice shaky.

Gray snatches his jacket from the back of the chair and heads for the door without a word.

Lange tries to reach him one last time. "Why are you so hell-bent on denying your truth?"

Gray stops with his hand on the doorknob and speaks without looking back. "My truth," he says. "Abo, bung, coon – I copped that and worse every day, at school, out playing, that was my truth".

Lange has a crushing sensation in his chest and takes a deep breath as he carefully chooses his next words. "I know it was hard on you, son, but you can't deny who you are". His voice falters on ragged breath. "That path only leads to more pain and darkness … Gray …"
Gray picks up his father's stressed tone and, realizing something is wrong, turns to face him. Lange instantly crumples like a rag doll onto the floor.

"Dad!" Gray rushes to his father's side and cradles him in his arms. The fall has opened up a nasty cut on Lange's forehead, and his face is matted with sawdust. His eye glazes over and a final breath rattles from his lungs. "Don't do this" pleads Gray. He quickly feels for a pulse and finds none. "No, no, no!" He frantically yells for help and hugs Lange tightly to his chest. "I've got you, Dad" he whispers as he gently brushes sawdust from Lange's face "You've cracked yourself a real beaut, but you'll be alright. "Help!" he yells again.

A curious neighbour nervously pokes her head into the garage and takes in the situation at a glance. "Lange, I heard - Oh god" she gasps.

"Call an ambulance, please, call an ambulance" Gray begs tearfully.

She hurries away to do as he asked, leaving Gray gently cradling his father in his arms.
⍰

CHAPTER 4

THE KING OF LOVE, MY SHEPHERD IS, sings the
congregation with enthusiasm. Their voices rise, muted,
from within the old brick-and-tile Holy Trinity church.

Inside the church, Father Roy Higgins stands at the
podium, Lange's coffin on the raised platform behind
him. He had married Lange and Beth in this very church
over forty years ago, so it seems only fitting that this is
where he should be farewelled.

The hymn comes to an end. "Please, be seated," he
instructs the congregation, and they all sit as one.

Gray and Robyn are seated in the front pew. A dozen
Indigenous elders enter the church and quietly take up
the back row of seats. Robyn acknowledges their
presence with a courteous nod and gets one in return.
Gray glances over the newcomers briefly, but recognizes
none of them.

"I would now ask Lange's only son, Gray, to say a few
words on behalf of the family".

Robyn squeezes his hand as he gets to his feet and
walks stiffly to the podium. Father Higgins places a
comforting hand on Gray's shoulder. "Just take your
time and breathe".

Gray inhales a deep breath and nods his head – got it. He takes a moment to look at the mourners' faces and to collect his thoughts.

"Last night I tried to write a list of the fine attributes my father had, but there were so many I didn't know where to start. I tried to write a few of the moments that described him as the man he was, but the moments were endless. So, I gave it up as impossible. I couldn't sum up his life on a page or two. But what I can tell you is how much it would have meant to him to know that his family and friends were here, because they were everything to him. Family meant everything to him. He'd say, when you have family you're never lonely, even when you're alone. When you hold someone in your mind, in your heart, to care for, to fight for, to dream for, near or far, broken or whole, they are your family, regardless. And now my father has gone and I am broken. Selfishly I will miss him, but he is with my mum now, where he always wanted to be." Gray turns towards the coffin and places his hand on the lid. "I'm sorry I let you down".

Father Higgins takes Gray's hand in a warm grip. "He was always proud of you, Gray" he tells him.

"I don't think so, Father" Gray replies, and returns to his seat beside Robyn. She puts her hand on his leg, a simple gesture of comfort that he barely notices.

His mind is filled with remorse over his final words with his father and the rest of the ceremony goes by in a blur of eulogies from friends and relatives until the benediction prayer. "Please stand" says Father Higgins. The mourners rise to their feet and he begins: "May the Lord bless you and keep you; the Lord makes his face shine upon you and be gracious unto you; the Lord turn his face toward you and give you peace". Organ music fills the church and the curtains draw across the coffin.

Gray and Robyn lead the mourners out of the church, the front rows going first and subsequent rows falling in behind them. Gray, Robyn and Father Higgins stand by the doors thanking the mourners as they slowly file out of the church. The group of Indigenous mourners are among the last to leave.

The eldest man stops while the others move on. He warmly shakes Robyn's hand and makes her the centre of his attention. "Please accept my condolences. Your father-in-law was a friend and wise council. I'm sorry we were late. We have one flight a day and the schedule is hit and miss at best".

Robyn smiles and turns to introduce the man to Gray "You got here and that's all that matters. This is my husband, Gray".

The man shifts his focus to Gray and holds out his hand at hip height "Gray, I haven't seen you since you were this tall".

Gray has no recollection of the man or of ever having met him "I'm sorry, have we met?

The man nods his head "A long time ago, yes. Your father wanted you to spend some time with us, but I suggested he wait".

Gray is curious "Wait, for..?"

"Until you were ready" the man solemnly replies.

Gray can't help the cynical smile appearing "Is this where I'm supposed to take the river pebbles from your hand to be truly ready?" He mocks.

Robyn is shocked by his overt sarcasm and disrespect "Gray!" She hisses.

"It's alright" says the man as he reaches out and takes Gray's forearm in a friendly but firm grip. "Caine was a foreigner in a foreign land. Our people are treated as foreigners in their own land. Us bush fellas watch TV, just like you city blokes, hey".

There's a moment of uncomfortable silence before Gray pulls his arm free from the man's grip.

"Look, I don't mean to sound disrespectful, but the whole, find yourself in the dreamtime, save it for the white tourists.

The Indigenous man remains eerily calm and this just seems to inflame Gray, so Robyn positions herself between the two men "I'm so sorry, this has been really hard on him and..."

Gray cuts her off mid-sentence. "Don't make excuses for me, Rob. You're not my bloody mother".

"No, I'm bloody well not, so stop acting like a child" She snaps back.

Everyone within earshot has stopped and is now watching them. Gray glances at the faces of the mourners. Some he's known all of his life; others are his father's old work colleagues, some he doesn't know at all, but right now he is inexplicably angered by all of them and just wants to mute out the world.

He walks away from Robyn and the Indigenous man and doesn't stop until he finds himself a few miles from the church. He weighs up his options – walk home or hail a cab? He raises his hand at the first empty cab he sees at the driver blatantly cruises past him "Fucker" he yells at the disappearing tail lights. He is luckier on the second attempt, hops into the back of the taxi, and tells the driver his address.

Gray arrives home in the dark, tiptoes into the house, and heads straight to bed. He quietly undresses in the dark so as not to wake Robyn, who's asleep with her back to him. He slips between the sheets and looks at Robyn's outline in the dim light. He wants to apologize, and silently admonishes himself – God, apologising is all I seem to do lately. Gray rolls onto his back, and the last thought in his mind before slipping into a troubled sleep is how much he loves her, and that he can do – no, has to do – better.

Robyn's eyes opened the moment she heard the key in the front door. Anger and despair have made her restless, and she is fast reaching her wits' end. She has spent far too much time questioning herself, blaming herself, for Gray's issues. She is aware that she's been a little more emotional of late, and that has translated to being snappy, but damn it, she needs Gray to step up now more than ever. She closes her eyes and chases the sleep that has thus far eluded her.

⁇

CHAPTER 5

THE DREAMING

THE SOUND OF A BULL-ROARER gently begins to build until it reaches a crescendo. Gray is lying belly down on the bank of a river, his body covered in thick mud, close to the brackish water. A series of bubbles break the surface and moves slowly, steadily, towards him. The tip of a massive estuarine crocodile's snout breaks the surface followed by the rest of its massive body as it slowly rises from the murky depths.

Gray remains motionless, frozen with fear, as the crocodile hauls its massive bulk onto the bank mere centimetres from Gray's face.

The crocodiles opens its jaws impossibly wide, giving Gray a view straight down its gullet, and freezing the blood in his veins.

Those powerful jaws slam closed with frightening speed and Gray screams.
⍰

CHAPTER 6

TWO GOLDEN-BROWN SLICES OF TOAST pop noisily out of the toaster. Robyn gingerly removes them and drops them onto a plate, as Gray slouches into the kitchen looking shattered.

He pours himself a coffee and slumps into a chair.

"Did you sleep?" she asks, placing the toast and a bottle of Vegemite on the table in front of him.

"Off and on. Still having the same weird dream" he replies, as he lathers the warm toast with butter and Vegemite.

She's only too aware of the stress he's been dealing with since Lange passed away a month ago and wants to share his burden, but any attempt at conversation only turns into an argument. Robyn places a copy of Time magazine on the table in front of him.

He searches the cover for a clue as to why he's being presented with the magazine, and then looks questioningly at her. "Time?"

"Just read," she says.

He picks it up and gives her the look again. "All of it? This could take a while."

"Page twelve" she says impatiently.

Gray flips through and finds a bulky page marker made up of two Qantas airline tickets taped to the page. He checks out the details. "Darwin?" he asks.

"Gove via Darwin," she replies.

He removes the tickets from the page and notes the story heading: "The Last Great Frontier – sounds like an episode of Star Trek. Rob, I can't–"

She cuts him off. "We leave Friday night."

He continues, "No, I can't just drop everything. I've got a backlog of cases."

But Robyn is having none of it. "The partners understand – in fact, they insisted. As of today you're on vacation. We arrive in Darwin on Saturday the twenty-first, switch flights to Gove, and fly back straight after New Year's Eve."

Gray plays with the food on his plate while he processes everything he's just been told.

"Did it occur to you that I might have wanted to be included in these conversations between my wife and my boss.?" His eyes remain glued to his food as he speaks.

The temperature in the room is rising and she tries to diffuse it. "Gray, we're all just worried about you".

He laughs. "Well, thank you for your concern, but I didn't ask for it, and I sure as hell don't need any time off". He shoves the plate across the table and kicks the chair back. "Don't ever go behind my back again Robyn".

He storms out of the kitchen; the front door slams and tears spill down her cheeks. She wipes them away and clears away the breakfast plates, then makes a mug of steaming-hot tea and takes it with her into her studio at the rear of the house. There's already a canvas on the easel with a partially completed painting of a fruit bowl.

The work is incredibly photorealistic. She picks her colours, loads her palette, and begins work. This is her refuge, where the world is kept at bay and her mind can reset.

⍰

CHAPTER 7

THE NEEDLE PUSHES PAST EIGHTY and the Porsche's engine roars as Gray shifts into fourth, drops the clutch, and floors the accelerator. The tyres squeal as he takes a bend at speed, and he fights the wheel for control. His mind is racing faster than the Porsche's engine – so many questions, but always coming back to one: Why am I always so angry? It's a question he's battled with answering for as long as he can remember, and one he's never been able to answer.

He left the city behind half an hour ago, and now it's open roads and trees flashing past as he pushes the Porsche past his capability to drive it.

Gray's thoughts flash back to the week after Lange died. He'd started boxing up his father's law books and had come across the first book that Lange had ever given him. Its subject was legal history, and inside the cover was a hand-written quote he'd forgotten was there: Not everything that is faced can be changed, but nothing can be changed until it is faced. – James Baldwin.

He wipes away the tears brimming in his eyes, momentarily loses his focus on the road, and enters a sharp corner too fast. The tyres scream and lose

31

contact. He throws the wheel into an opposing lock to steer through the ensuing slide, but it's too late.
The Porsche slews sideways onto the dirt shoulder and spins three-sixty, narrowly missing any trees, and finally comes to a shuddering halt in a cloud of billowing dust.

Gray turns the ignition key to shut down the engine, but it's already stalled. He pulls on the handbrake, climbs out, and glances around to see if there are any witnesses to his stupidity but he is alone on this stretch of road. His thoughts go to Robyn, the one good thing in his life and he's pushing her away. "What's wrong with you?" he screams into the void and waits for an answer that he knows can only come from within. He climbs back into the vehicle, fires it up, and sedately heads back the way he came.

CHAPTER 8

ROBYN IS LOST IN HER WORK when Gray returns. She doesn't hear the car pull up, or the front door open, but she's aware of his presence when he enters her studio and purposefully ignores him.

He comes up behind her and places his hands on her waist. She stiffens straight away "Rob, I'm so sorry".

She places her brush on the palette, but doesn't turn to face him.

He wraps his arms around her, presses his chest to her back, and whispers into her ear, "I'm a dick. Please forgive me." He kisses her neck and she trembles at his touch.

"Bastard," she moans, and then turns to face him. "Say it again?"

He looks deeply into her eyes. "I'm a dick. Please forgive me." He continues, "Gove, huh?"

She takes over. "The tribal land of your mother's people, the Yolngu."

"So, it's not them fellas down at the pub, then?" he asks with mock sincerity.

This gets a smile from her. "We'll see out seventy-four in style, and welcome in seventy-five under the stars."

He kisses her neck again. "Okay, you win. But I'm drawing the line at sampling the local foods. No grubs, lizard, or snake for this black fella. Deal?"

"Deal" she mimics, and returns his kiss passionately.
▯

CHAPTER 9

THE STORM

ON THE RADAR SCREEN, a swirling mass sits to the west, northwest of Bathurst Island. Gary Holland's focus doesn't waver from the screen as he takes a half dozen photographs with a Polaroid camera.

He locks up behind him as he leaves, and drives the fifteen minutes from the radar installation at the airport to the Met Office in Darwin's CBD. He parks his car under an overhang of the ten-storey building, hurries inside, and takes the elevator up to the eighth floor.

Geoff Crane and Ray Wilkie are both working at their desks. "You might want to take a look at these" Gary says to Geoff, and tosses the photos onto his desk. "She's a big bugger" says Geoff. "What's her name?"

Gary glances at Ray and grins. "What was the name of that hellcat you brought to the Christmas function last week?"

Ray searches his memory, picks up a pen, writes Tracy on a sheet of paper, and holds it up for both of them to see.

"What's Tracy's current heading?" Geoff asks.
Gary crosses to a wall map and traces Tracy's current path with his finger. "South, southeast. Moving at four KPH. She should hit the Tiwi Islands day after tomorrow."

Geoff as he leans back in his chair and studies the map. He's no idiot and takes his job seriously, but during their time in the Top End they've seen dozens of cyclones and they never amount to much. Tracy will probably be no different he thinks to himself. "We'll keep tracking her, but I doubt we'll see much from her" Gary articulates his thoughts with reasonable certainty. After all, Selma had recently sailed past. Maybe they were blessed. "Alright, it's beer o'clock," he calls out. "Ray, if you'll do the honours?"

Ray opens the fridge, pulls out three beers, and passes them out. They pop the tabs. "Cheers," echo all three, and they each take a long swig.

The light from the window strikes the Polaroids at just the right angle to create the illusion of movement. Geoff catches the anomaly in his peripheral vision and it sends an inexplicable shiver up his spine that's forgotten as quickly as it came.
⬚

CHAPTER 10

"IT LOOKS LIKE THE EARTH IS BLEEDING" says Robyn, as she gazes down on it from 10,000 feet. She nudges Gray and points to the window. "Take a look".

He leans over her and gazes out. "It's very ... red" he says with little enthusiasm.

She pushes him back into his seat and shakes her head in disgust. "It's incredible".

The ten-year-old boy in the seat adjacent to Gray's sneaks curious glances at him from his seat. Gray catches him, and grins disarmingly. The boy slowly smiles back, until his mother puts an end to the game.

Robyn excitedly grabs him by the arm. "Oh, wow, look at this".

He leans over her again to look out of the window. Far below lies the Nabalco plant site. Smoke pours out of towering stacks and row upon row of huge storage tanks dominate the landscape. "It looks like a wound in the earth" he says sadly, and she agrees. There are massive man-made pools of waste sludge across from the plant, and a road between them that leads to the town of Nhulunbuy some twenty kilometres away.

Robyn pushes her face tightly against his so she can see the view. "The Bauxite they mine here is transported to container ships on the longest conveyor belt in the Southern Hemisphere" she informs him.

"Is that right?" he asks.

"As a matter of fact, yes, it is. And all of it Indigenous land, leased by the mining company" she adds.

Beyond the plant site they can see the ship loader, connected to the mine fifteen kilometres away by a covered conveyor belt cutting through the native bush.
⍰

CHAPTER 11

THE SUN BEATS DOWN ON A FOUR-MAN CREW
replacing bearings on the ship loader. Hopkins tightens
a locking nut on a bearing assembly. He listens to his
Greek co-workers chatting away to each other and
watches as they pass around cigarettes they've been
sent from relatives in Greece.

Hopkins firmly believes that if you come to Australia,
you speak the Queen's fucking English. On any other day
he could let it slide, but he'd had a letter from the ex-
wife's lawyer yesterday restricting access to his
daughters, so today is not one of those days. "Do you
lazy bastards do anything, I mean, other than smoke
that stink-weed you call tobacco and arse fuck each
other?" he asks.

The Greeks look at him with little to no comprehension,
and this pisses him off more. "Learn to speak English or
fuck off back to wog land, you dopey cunts". He
punctuates the statement with a clang as he drops the
spanner into his toolkit.

One of the Greeks has enough of a grasp of English to
understand a little. "Eh fungool pusti malaka" he spits,
and this gets a nervous laugh from his friends who know
this literally means "Fuck you wanker".

Hopkins stares coldly at the man, stopping just short of launching at him, as the roar of a low-flying aircraft catches his attention. He leans precariously over the railing to get a better look and shades his eyes against the sun with his hand. The ocean shimmers more than fifty metres below him. A fall from this height would probably be fatal.

The Fokker Friendship passes overhead, the sun glinting off its fuselage. Hopkins watches it drop into its approach run before returning his attention to the smiling Greek guy. "Pass me out the twenty-inch crescent" he orders. The Greek guy doesn't respond.

Hopkins nudges the lid of the toolbox with his boot. "You don't understand or are you just fucking thick?" Hopkins watches as the Greek crouches down and reaches into the toolbox, and then drives the lid down with his boot trapping his hand. Blood flows as the skin is torn and he cries out in pain. His friends move to help, but hesitate as Hopkins pushes the lid down harder . "Not so fucking lippy now, are you?" he snarls.

The look in Hopkins' eyes terrifies the Greek. He holds out his free hand to motion his friends to back off and to show his submission to Hopkins. "Please, English next time" he says through gritted teeth.

It takes a moment before Hopkins reins in his anger and removes his boot from the lid.

"You should get that looked at." He says with mock concern as the Greek pulls out his bloody hand and cradles it to his chest. Hopkins closes the toolbox and picks it up "A nasty cut like that could get infected". He strides down the access stairs all calls back over his shoulder "You could lose your hand".

The Greeks comfort their friend and pour fresh water from a flask over his wounded hand. They watch Hopkins making his way down the ramp with burning hatred in their eyes – If looks could kill.

CHAPTER 12

THE PLANE BLOCKS OUT THE SUN as it passes overhead, and Anthony Johannson gives it a cursory glance before turning his gaze back the dozen topless young boys, dressed in scout shorts and shoes, cleaning the outside of the scout hall with brooms and a fire hose. He snaps off picture after picture from a Polaroid camera, capturing images of water splashing tanned skin, the boys wrestling over the hose, and suds flying in all directions as they try to soak each other.

Johannson grew up in Adelaide, South Australia, with straight-laced, religious parents. He always knew he was different, particularly in his sexual preferences. His first encounter as a child was with his local priest. There was no fear – in fact, he embraced it. He embraced the pain of penetration as though it were a rite of passage. It seemed to him as natural as any love could be, but the priest warned him that others wouldn't see it in the same light and told him that he must keep it their secret. Over the years, Johannson became good at keeping secrets, which served him well, because now there were so many of them.

He came to Gove in seventy-two and worked as a cook, but it offered him no chances to satisfy his urges. He'd been a scout master in Adelaide, but he had been made to leave under a cloud after sexual misconduct allegations were brought against him.

The boys in question were terrified that once the story got out, they'd be labelled as queers, so even though it ate them up inside, they stayed silent. Nothing had be proved, but Johannson still thought it prudent to get as far away as possible.

Johannson started the first Scout troop in Nhulunbuy and played his hand slowly. The parents thought of him as a little eccentric, but essentially harmless. He took his time patiently grooming his boys and supplying them with Ganja to make them more compliant. He told them that they were a part of something special that no one else would understand and the secret had to be kept between them.

?

CHAPTER 13

"CRASH AND BURN, YOU FUCKERS" whispers Brett
'Scotty' Scott, as he targets the Fokker Friendship with
his makeshift two-fingered sights. He's lying on his back,
a half-eaten sandwich in one hand, beside the crusher
he and his workmate, Martin 'Marty' Wilks are
supposed to be servicing.

Scotty likes to refer to himself as a Govite, but he was
born and bred in Tasmania. He came from a family of
nine and vanished among his siblings. His school years
were similar – just one of the crowd with nothing to
make him stand out, other than his flaming red hair, and
a way-below-average education. When he got the job in
Gove he thought it would be the making of him, but he
just ended up disappearing again. It was only meeting
Hopkins that changed things for him. He became a part
of a dysfunctional family, learnt a new ideology, and
gained an overwhelming desire to be like his surrogate
father.

He watches Wilks finish loading up the wheelbarrow.
"Feel free to give us a hand anytime," Wilks says snidely
to Scotty, as he sets the shovel aside and wipes the
sweat from his eyes.

Wilks – long, lean, shaggy haired – is a few years
younger than Scotty and originally from Perth. He'd got
into trouble with the law a few times growing up.

It wasn't that he was a bad guy, but he's always been a follower, never a leader. Having an undiagnosed mental issue didn't help either, but he managed to hide it better as he got older. Gove was a chance for him to leave his past and his troubles behind – but the one thing you always take with you is yourself, and he quickly slid into the same patterns of peer group dependency.

Scotty looks from his half-eaten sandwich. "I'm on me fuckin' lunch break, mate."

Wilks shakes his head in resignation. "Your lunch breaks would make the Guinness Book of Records."

"Right up there with your fuckin' whinging," Scotty retorts.

Wilks flashes him the bird, and as he drops his hand, catches his wristwatch on the handle, shattering the glass face. "Fuck it" he quietly curses, undoes the watch strap, and pockets it to minimize any further damage. He's angry at himself for damaging the only gift his mother had ever given him, along with a solemn piece of advice: "If you're stupid it'll get you killed. You'll die stupid. Understand?" Her words echo in his head as he pushes the wheelbarrow up the ramp.

Wilksy, you are not the brightest crayon in the colouring box, Scotty thinks to himself as he swats most of the flies away from his sandwich and takes a bite. Bread, sausage and flies all blend together between his teeth. He washes it down with swig of ice-cold Coke from his esky and resumes doing what he does best – nothing.

?

CHAPTER 14

THE LANDING GEAR LOWERS and there's a loud
mechanical thud as it locks into place. The Fokker
touches down and taxis towards the terminal – nothing
more than a large, demountable site building. Beyond
the fence is a large sign: WELCOME TO NHULUNBUY,
NORTHERN TERRITORY.

The passengers disembark, with Gray and Robyn near
the front of the queue. The airport staff are quick to
unload the bags and Avis already have their four-wheel-
drive gassed and ready to. Now it's a simple matter of
retrieving their luggage and following the signs towards
Nhulunbuy.

Robyn drives, while Gray gazes out of the window at the
passing scenery. He flicks the air-conditioning up to
high. "Jesus, it's hot. You could fry an egg on the
bonnet," he complains.

The fenced-in wreckage of a WW2 bomber flashes past.
Gray finds this amusing. "I think somebody missed the
runway".

Robyn flashes it a look. "It's a memorial. There were
airfields hidden all over this area during the Second
World War. Gove Peninsula was actually named after
William Gove, an RAAF navigator killed in a mid-air
collision".

Gray looks impressed. "Someone's done their homework".

Robin laughs, pulls a tourist information brochure from the door pocket and hands it to him. "Knock yourself out".

They cruise past a dusty road sign that reads: Nhulunbuy Town Centre 18 km. Twenty minutes later they turn right and pass a hospital on the left.

They crest a rise, cruising towards the town centre and out the other side, where the sparkling Arafura Sea comes into view. "Wow." Gray is in awe. "That's beautiful". His face lights up. "Let's check in and then go for a swim" he says enthusiastically.

She smiles and pats his hand. "Okay, but first we need to have a talk about the really big saltwater crocodiles".

The smile slides from his face. "The really big what..?" He looks like a kid that just found out Santa Claus isn't real, and she can't help bursting into laughter.

⍰

CHAPTER 15

GRAVEL CRUNCHES BENEATH THE TYRES as Robyn
brings the four-wheel-drive to a standstill outside the
Walkabout Hotel. She goes into the reception area while
Gray unloads the bags.

A group of young Aboriginal girls meander past, giggling
and chirping away in their own tongue. One of them, a
pretty young Yolngu girl, catches Gray's eye and smiles
at him. He returns the smile and accidentally drops one
of the suitcases onto his foot. "Shit!" he yelps. The girls
laugh out loud and move on.

He takes a moment to take in the lie of the land. There's
a service station off to his left, and the main bar of the
pub to his right. Across the street are the fire
department and a shopping centre. Pretty place.

Robyn watches as the receptionist runs her finger down
the page of the guest ledger. "Garrett." She runs her
finger down the next page, "Garrett – Gray and Robyn.
Here we are." She removes a room key from a hook on a
near-empty board. "I'll bet this is a welcome change
from Melbourne weather," she says, handing over the
key.

Robyn signs the guest book and takes the key. "Is it
always this humid?" she asks, wiping the sweat from her
brow.

"Only two seasons in the Territory – wet and dry – and you're here smack bang in the middle of the wet" replies the receptionist with a smile.

Gray pushes through the reception doors, a suitcase in each hand, staggering under the weight. "Please tell me we're on the bottom floor," he says to Robyn, then turns to the receptionist. "G'day".

She seems momentarily taken aback, but quickly regains her composure.

"This is my husband, Gray" says Robyn.

He drops the bags. "And part-time pack mule" he says with a grin. "Is it always this humid?"

Robyn and the receptionist laugh out loud.

"What did I say?" he asks, confused.

Robyn pats his chest. "It's the wet season. Don't you know anything?" Robyn and the receptionist share a smile.

"Let's get you folks to your room and turn on the aircon before you melt," says the receptionist. "Follow me, please." She leads them past an ornate Christmas tree, and the stairs leading up to the restaurant.

"The restaurant's back the way we came," she says, unlocking their room, "upstairs above reception."

Gray drops the suitcases beside the bed, shakes out his aching arms.

They check out the room. Basic, but comfortable.

"The pool is just outside, in the courtyard. Anything else you need, just call reception. Enjoy your stay with us."

She leaves, and Gray dives across the bed, flicks on the air-conditioner, and turns the temperature control to frosty. "I'm not moving further than the bathroom, unless it's to another air-conditioned room or the pool," he says as he flops onto his back.

Robyn hauls her case onto the bed, beside him. "Harden up, mister. You're in the Territory now".

"Where the men are men and the water buffalo are nervous" he replies with a smirk.

She picks up the nearest pillow and beats him with it. He snatches it from her and hurls it at her. She leaps on him, giggling, and pins him down. He could dislodge her easily, but he likes the feel of her body against his. "We needed this, Gray. It's going to be a great experience". He moves between her legs and she can feel how hard he is.

She pushes her hips up and grinds against him again. He slowly undoes the buttons of her top, exposing her creamy white breasts and hardening nipples. She moans, and peels his shirt from his shoulders. Gray pulls her shorts and panties down with one hand and her helping hands. She unzips him and gasps as he drives into her. Their love-making is intense, noisy, and brief. It's been a couple of months since they've bonded on this level. They climax quickly, collapse in a tangled, sweaty mess, and fall asleep in each other's arms.

⏎

CHAPTER 16

"DADDY'S HOME! DADDY'S HOME!" Hopkins smiles at the sound of the voice echoing in his memory. His daughters, nine-year-old Sarah, who wants to be a veterinarian when she grows up, and seven-year-old Alison, who wants to be a cat, are bouncing up and down on their beds in excitement. He can see the flurry of colour and movement in his mind's eye, but that quickly fades into the reality of the two single beds with their bare mattresses and the closet doors open, bare coat hangers dangling from the rail. In this moment he feels the same visceral pain he felt on the day he lost them.

He turns away from the empty closet and turns towards the stark, gloomy dining room. Sarah's voice drifts on the air. "What is it, Daddy?" A large cardboard box is perched on the dining table. His girls are staring at it, burning with curiosity.

Hopkins can see Sharon watching from the kitchen in his peripheral vision, her expression guarded. Over the years, she's learnt to keep her emotions and responses close to her chest. Better to wait until she's worked out his mood before doing anything that could set him off. This has been getting harder and harder to navigate; her life has become a balancing act; she's constantly walking on eggshells. But she has a plan, and part of that involves keeping him calm and unsuspecting.

Alison squeals, "What's in the box, Daddy? What, Daddy, what?"

He makes a show of studying their faces. "I don't know. Do you really want to see it?"

The girls grab a hand each and pull him towards the table. "Daddy, don't be silly," they admonish.

"Really?" he asks.

"Really!" they yell.

They release their grip on him and he tears open the box. He lifts out a new television with a flourish. "Ta da!" He places it on the table and plugs it in.

"It's television" they chime, unimpressed.

Hopkins weaves his hands over the television like a cheap vaudeville magician. "True, but not just any television. This one is magic".

They chorus together, "Silly, Daddy, televisions aren't magic".

Hopkins grips the power knob, says the magic word, "Abracadabra" and flicks on the power. The screen bursts into full colour, and the girls gasp in wonder. This is the first time they've seen TV in colour.

Sesame Street is playing, and a bright-yellow Big Bird is chatting with a purple Grover.

"Big bird is yellow," they whisper in unison.

Hopkins laughs and glances past the girls to Sharon, but the blank look on her face just irritates him. Nothing makes that sour cunt happy, he thinks to himself. Well, fuck her. She's not going to wreck this moment like she's managed to wreck so many others.

A black presenter appears on the screen and Alison giggles.

"What's so funny, baby?" asks Sharon.

"Niggers are the same in colour, Momma" she replies, that cute smile still on her face.

Sharon snaps, "Your room – now!"

Alison is confused and the smile slips from her face. "But, Momma…"

"Now!" yells Sharon.

Alison bursts into tears and hurries to her room with Sarah following closely behind.

Hopkins waits until their bedroom door shuts. "When did we started punishing the kids for honesty?"

"Do you hear yourself? Do you? You sound just like him". Sharon's tone is indignant and it instantly raises his hackles. The look he gives her makes her choose her next words carefully. "Please, Greg, we came here to get away from all of that. Look – you've been working so many hours lately. I thought it'd be nice to give you a break. How about I take the girls home to Mum and Dad, just for a couple of weeks, give you some space?"

"Really? And where do I pull the money from for that – out of my arse?" He goes into the kitchen, rips open the fridge, and grabs a beer, leaning into the fridge. The cold air washes over his face.

"I've been putting a little of my money away for a rainy day" she tells him.

He glances up at her and smiles thinly. "Your money?"

She tries to smile, but her bottom lip begins to quiver, and tears well in her eyes. "Please, Greg, I want to take them home, just for…"

He slams the fridge door. "This is our home" he growls. "We've built a fucking life here".

The tears spill down her cheeks. "You've built a life here," she whispers.

He cups his ear with his hand. "Speak up, you stupid cow".

She is shaking like a leaf. "This place. The drinking ..." She lets her words hang in the air. "The other women".

His gaze remains cold and unwavering.

"You think I don't know?" she asks.

His reply is as cold as his attitude. "No, Sharon, I just couldn't give a shit". He chugs the beer.

"Our tickets are booked" she says, trying to sound strong, but her voice still breaks. "We're going. You can visit them, but they're not coming back here".

He slams his beer down onto the table, grabs the new television, and hurls it across the room. Big Bird fills the screen until the plug rips from the socket. The television hits the far wall and shatters. "I break my fuckin' back working to support this family," he roars, now in a blinding rage.

He advances on her, and she backpedals, now terrified. "Greg ..." she pleads.

He backhands her across the kitchen. "You fucking ungrateful cunt."

She hits the floor with a thud and crawls into a corner, blood seeping from her nose and lip. "Get out – go to your mate's, go to your whores" she screams.

He grabs her by the throat, drags her to her feet, and slams her against the sink. Sharon gasps for breath and claws at his hand. "I've called my mother. She knows I'm leaving you. If you hurt me …" she wheezes.

His eyes bore into hers as he speaks "The worst mistake I ever made was to choose you over my family" His grip tightens.

Her next words are strangled and barely audible. "You'll never see the girls from jail".

This breaks through the rage barrier, and he loosens his grip enough that she can draw in a breath.

"Daddy, please, no" He glances over his shoulder and sees the girls standing behind him, tears streaming down their cheeks, terrified. He takes his hand from Sharon's throat and she gasps in air. She shoves him out of the way, gathers the girls into her arms, and sits on the floor with them.

Hopkins rips open the fridge, grabs another beer and heads for the front door, then pauses. He pointedly clocks the three hunting rifles mounted, chained, and padlocked, above the master bedroom door. He fishes his keys from his pocket. His eyes remain focused on the rifles as he holds up the keys and rattles them. "Don't push me, Sharon".

Sharon is well aware that the keys to the locks securing the rifles are in that bunch, and she clearly understands his intent. This isn't the first time he's threatened her, but it is the first time that the threat has been terminal.

He hammers through the front door and slams it behind him, leaving Sharon, Sarah, and Alison, sobbing as they cling together.

The colour leaches out of the room and the sobbing fades to whimpers, and Hopkins is alone in the lounge room with his thoughts again. The phantom sound of a vehicle in the driveway draws him across to the window. He gazes out at the overgrown yard and the rusty swing set, standing as a constant reminder of his girls. In his mind's eye, night turns to day again.

A taxi with a police escort pulls away from the house, with Sarah and Alison looking tearfully back at him through the rear window. He can see the fear in their eyes, and his anger builds all over again. She did this, his mind screams, she turned my kids against me.

He regrets not killing her while he had the chance, but there will come a time, and he's a patient man.

The vehicles round the corner and disappear from sight, leaving only a cloud of dust in their wake. The memory dissolves as day becomes night again. He turns his back on the overgrown yard, the swing set, the family he left his country of birth and his parents for. He crosses the room to the photograph of his father, and lifts it from the hook. "I'm sorry, dad." Tears well in his eyes. He removes the back of the frame and carefully peels out the photograph. He runs his fingers along the distinct fold line at the top. "You were right" he whispers, as he unfolds the portion of the photograph hidden by the fold and places it face up on the cabinet. The name above the shop window is painted in bold black letters on a stark white background: The White Défense League.

CHAPTER 17

THE DREAMING

THE EERIE SOUND OF THE BULL-ROARER fills the air.
Gray is standing on the bank of the same river. The sun
glistens off the surface, creating magical prisms of
dancing light. Every fibre of his being screams at him to
stay out of the water, but his body disobeys and he
wades into the river. When he's waist deep he dives
beneath the surface. Even under water, the sound of
the bull-roarer builds, resonating inside his skull.

He swims through the murky water, scanning for
danger, but visibility is low, and his fear levels are
climbing. The bull-roarer reaches a crescendo. The big
crocodile glides through the water towards him. Gray's
eyes bulge and he freezes in terror. The crocodile
thrusts its muscular tail, increases its speed
dramatically, turns onto its side, and opens those
powerful jaws. Gray screams, and bubbles explode from
his mouth.

⁇

CHAPTER 18

GRAY'S EYES SNAP OPEN. The dream felt so real and he struggles to orientate himself. The room is in total darkness, which doesn't help his growing anxiety. He blindly reaches out, feeling for Robyn; she's still fast asleep beside him. Her warmth and presence calm him and it slowly dawns on him that he's in the hotel room. He picks up his watch from the bedside table and checks the time: eight p.m. He climbs out of bed, quietly carries his suitcase into the bathroom, and closes the door. A couple of minutes later he reappears, dressed in jeans, a polo shirt and a pair of loafers. Gray switches off the light and quietly slips out of the room.

He moves along the corridor towards the reception. The dull sound of raised voices and rock music come from the bar.

The cigarette-smoke-filled bar is packed with drunken men he assumes are miners and contractors, plus a smattering of hard-looking women. Tables are laden with jugs of beer and perpetually full glasses. Most of the miners are dressed in their work clothes – a mix of khaki shirts, long pants or khaki shorts, and blue singlets. All are dirt and grease stained. The pool table and jukebox take up the back quarter of the room. A record drops and 'Billy Don't be a Hero' begins to play.

The side of the pool table is lined with coins from the challengers. A dozen or so men watch on as Hopkins and Scotty battle it out on the table. Hopkins lines up the black ball with Johannson just behind on his cue side.

"Easy shot, mate. It's all yours," encourages Johannson.

Hopkins has plenty of room to take the shot, but listening to Johannson's voice is like chewing on tinfoil. He deliberately and forcefully drives the cue back, catching Johannson solidly on the hip bone, causing him to yelp in pain. "You're putting me off my shot," says Hopkins.

"Sorry, I just–" replies Johannson.

"Need to shut the fuck up," growls Hopkins.

Johannson slips back behind the other onlookers to cover his embarrassment.

Hopkins lines up the shot again, and Scotty manoeuvres himself into his line of sight.

"Pressure gettin' to ya, mate?" says Scotty. "Take the bloody shot already."

Hopkins draws the cue back over his knuckles. "It's all over bar the shouting, pup,"

Scotty sneers "You won't sink this, mate. There's no fuckin' hair around the hole."

Hopkins slowly breathes out, like a sniper about to squeeze the trigger. "Hole's ..." he drives the cue smoothly across the bridge of his hand, "a hole." The white ball slams into the black ball, spearing it into the top right corner pocket.

Scotty cries out in anguish. "Fuckin' cunt!"

Hopkins passes him his empty glass. "Schooner of Carlton." To the waiting men: "Next?"

One of the other miners picks up the first coins in the row, inserts them into the coin slot, and racks the balls.

Gray enters and heads straight to the bar, oblivious to the stares of almost every patron in the place. He signals for the barman, and clocks the miners leaning against the bar staring at him. "G'day, fellas," he says politely. They don't respond, and move further away.

The barman delivers a couple of beers to the miners closest to Gray.

"Any chance of getting a coldy?" calls Gray. "Anything's fine as long as it's wet". The barman doesn't even look his way. He shouts to be heard. "This year would be good".

The barman finally approaches him, leans across the bar, and bluntly says, "Mate, turn around and leave, before there's any trouble". Gray smiles, thinking it's a joke, but the unfaltering look on the barman's face says otherwise.

Someone pulls out the jukebox power cord and the music dies with a slur of lyrics.

A miner calls out from across the bar, "You lost, Jackie, Jackie?"

Gray turns towards the two men coming towards him.

"Made a wrong turn on the way to the reserve?" says the other miner. The men laugh, and Gray laughs along with them. Right now it's just harmless fun at his expense. Why turn it into something else? he rationalizes. Keep it light. "I'm just in for a coldy. Didn't mean to interrupt anything," he says, still smiling.

The first miner moves through the crowd with the second in tow. "Well, listen to this, an educated coon". He's playing to his audience. "Where are you from, your Lordship?"

Gray refuses to be baited. "Melbourne," he replies, holding out his hand. "Name's Gray."

The gesture goes ignored, and the second miner snorts a laugh. "Fuckin' hell – Gray – that's a shade of black, isn't it?" The miners laugh loudly and the speaker takes a bow.

The first miner inches closer. "Doesn't the Victorian government think we've got enough blacks of our own? Now they're exporting theirs up here too?"

The barman has one eye on the miner while he rummages beneath the counter for something. "Hopkins ..." he warns.

Gray now thinks a tactical retreat would be better than a physical beating – live to fight another day and all that shit races through his mind. "I'm not looking for any trouble. I'll just leave you fellas to it" he says, taking a step back towards the exit.

Hopkins takes a couple of slow menacing steps past Gray, cutting him off. "What, now we're not good enough to drink with?" he asks, his tone offended.

The barman pulls out the peace-keeper – a well-worn, blood-stained cricket bat, and pointedly thumps it onto the bar. "I'm warning you ..."

But Hopkins seems well past caring about warnings. "Look, all I was trying to do was get a beer, mate". Gray's tone is still friendly.

Hopkins accelerates from zero to blind rage in an instant. "I am not your fuckin' mate, you black cunt" he screams into Gray's face, and swings a vicious hay-maker.

Gray ducks, barely managing to avoid the blow, and instinctively responds with a jab that rocks Hopkins, draws blood, that only serves to fuel his rage further. Gray is aware that the whole pack could turn on him in a flash, and defensively backs up against the bar.

Hopkins squares off and moves in to throw another punch, but the peace-keeper is thrust under his chin and he is brought up short. He tries to swat it aside, but the barman is ready for him and deftly avoids the move. Hopkins turns his eyes on the barman with vicious intent.

"Try it. I'll knock you for a bloody six" The barman's a big guy and he is deadly serious.

Hopkins spits out the words, "Fuckin' coon lover".

The barman jams the cricket bat harder under Hopkins' chin. "Not in here, dickhead. Got it?"

Hopkins is furious, but grudgingly, and wisely, keeps his mouth shut.

The barman keeps his eyes locked on Hopkins while directing his words to Gray. "If you still want that beer, go out the back to the coon – garden – bar".

Gray nods his thanks to the barman and slowly backs towards the exit.

"Yeah, out back with the rest of the fucking mob" growls Hopkins.

"Thanks for the hospitality" says Gray. "No, don't worry ..." A big hairy miner makes a point of bumping him as he passes. "Y'all enjoy the rest of the clan meeting". He backs out the door and tosses them the bird as it closes behind him.

The barman slowly lowers the peace-maker. "You – have another beer and cool down" he says to Hopkins, and then addresses everyone else. "The rest of you bastards settle down or I'll close the bar early. I fuckin' mean it" he adds for emphasis.

The men break up and go back to their drinks. The drone of a dozen conversations starts up again. Someone plugs the jukebox back in and the end of 'Billy Don't be a Hero' slurs back up to speed.

"Well, am I gonna get any more grief out of you?" the barman asks Hopkins.

In reply, Hopkins spits a wad of blood and phlegm onto the floor.

The barman shakes his head in resignation, goes back behind the bar, and returns the peace-maker to its original spot.

Wilks strolls out of the toilet doing up his fly, oblivious to the events that have taken place, and reeking of the ganja he's just smoked. He wipes his hands on his jeans and slouches over to Hopkins and Scotty. "What'd I miss?" he slurs.

Scotty glances from his bleary eyes to his shoe. "The trough," he casually observes. "You've pissed on ya fuckin' shoes".

Wilks bites, hook line and sinker, and looks at his shoes. They're bone dry. Scotty shakes his head and laughs. "Fuckin' dickhead. Did you catch that?" he says to Hopkins, but Hopkins is distracted, staring out of the window at the darkness beyond. His eyes are cold, unreadable, as he wipes away the blood from his split lip.

⏹

CHAPTER 19

THE GARDEN BAR IS POORLY LIT and dotted with ant-eaten wooden garden furniture. Three Indigenous men play the didgeridoo and clap sticks while one drunkenly sings and dances. A half-dozen drunken, full-blood, Indigenous men and women sit on the floor, bench seats, anywhere they can. All of them are drinking Victoria Bitter straight from the can, or cheap cask wine. The bar itself is nothing more than a besser-block box with a window and a metal roller door. A weary, battle-tested, middle-aged barmaid serves with all the enthusiasm of a wet dishcloth.

Gray carefully negotiates his way to the bar through the furniture and smattering of drinkers. The barmaid barely acknowledges his presence. "Yep?" she says, without taking her eyes off the local newspaper. "A beer would be a good end to a shit night," he replies. The barmaid is caught off guard by his voice, and looks a little stunned. "Melbourne, lawyer, married, in my forties. Have I missed anything?"

The barmaid's face lights up and she laughs. "I'm sorry," she says. "We don't get a lot like you in here".

Gray glances at the other patrons. "Black?" he asks.

"Funny," she replies. "Now, what can I get you?"

He smiles at her. "Thank you. All I want is a cold beer".

Twenty feet away, an old Indigenous woman, milky eyes, weathered skin, dirty frock, blearily eyes Gray from head to toe. "Ga' ngarali?" From her gesture, he deduces she's asking for a cigarette.

The barmaid pulls a can of VB out of the fridge and holds her hand out for the money. "That'll be two-fifty." Gray hands her the money and she hands him the can. "A glass?" he asks.

The old Indigenous woman weaves her way closer. "Ga' rrupiyah?" She's now clearly asking for money, and again she's ignored.

"Can I get a glass?" he repeats.

The barmaid shakes her head. "Clearly you're not from around here. No glasses in the garden bar. The abos – sorry, they end up using them as weapons against each other. It's the rules. It's a can or nothing".

He takes the can, cracks the ring-tab, and takes a long drink. The ice cold beer hits the spot and he savours that first hit before scoping out the rest of the bar. "Is it always this quiet?" he asks the barmaid.

"Not since I've been working here. Something's got them spooked," she replies.

The old Indigenous woman staggers over and stands unsteadily beside Gray. "Ga' ngarali?" she asks again.

"I'm sorry," Gray annunciates. "I can't understand you." The barmaid translates. "She wants a dowry. Don't give her anything or you'll never get rid of her," she warns.

The old woman gazes blearily into his eyes, before reaching out and rubbing his arm "There a white fella under there? Come out, white fella. Go marrtjina."

Gray pulls away from her, disgusted by her appearance and smell, and somewhere deep down, an irrational fear rises.

"Here." He hastily pulls out a ten dollar note from his pocket and tosses it at her. "Take it." It bounces off her chest and falls to the ground.

The old woman quickly covers the money with her foot, without taking her eyes off him. Her face turns into a scowl and she points a gnarly, weaving, finger at his face. "Not black fella, nah. Not white fella neither." She pokes him in the chest with her finger and it shocks him to the core. "You got no mob. You lost," she whispers.

Gray backs away from her, leaving his beer on the bar. "Nowhere man," she cackles, and every drunken eye in the place turns towards Gray.

He can feel them looking at him. He shrinks beneath their gaze and feels like he's on the outside for the second time tonight.

"He's coming for you. Namarrkon is coming, Nowhere Man" she drunkenly slurs, pointing into the night sky.

Gray turns away from the woman, away from the knowing looks, and flees the garden bar.

"Oi, what about your beer?" the barmaid calls after him, but she's talking to empty space. "Suit your bloody self". She reaches for the beer to bin it, but the old woman beats her to it.

"Yaka, ga," and she snatches the can from the bar with a speed that belies her drunken state. She skulls half of it in one go, before unsteadily picking up the money from beneath her foot. She mumbles to herself, "Storm's coming for you, Nowhere man. Namarrkon, he coming," and slaps the money down on the bar for four more beers. Once she has them she weaves her way out of the garden bar and heads for the beach to find a spot to make camp for the night.

?

CHAPTER 20

A BLINDING LIGHT PIERCES THE DARKNESS and Gray is caught in the glare halfway between the bar and the reception. The roar of an engine echoes across the car park. Tyres squeal and the lights leap forward. Gray is forced to dive out of the way or be hit, and lands hard on the gravel.

A short-wheel-base, rag-top Toyota Land Cruiser, tricked out with a roll bar and spotlights, roars past. "Get off the road, ya fuckin' black cunt" yells the person riding shotgun, as they speed past.

Gray catches a fleeting glimpse of Hopkins at the wheel before the vehicle reaches the street and disappears around a corner. He slowly, painfully, climbs to his feet; blood immediately soaks through his shirt and jeans. "Fuck." He limps towards the reception area, pushes through the door. "Are you alright?" asks the nightshift receptionist. He waves her off to avoid any fuss, and makes his way to his room.

Gray quietly enters and limps straight to the bathroom. He closes the door and a moment later, a slither of light appears. Robyn opens the bathroom door and finds him picking gravel from some nasty looking cuts and abrasions on his leg, through the tear in his jeans. "Sorry babe, I didn't mean to wake you," he says quietly, through gritted teeth.

She is far less restrained in her response. "Oh, my God – what happened?" She grabs a face cloth, wets it in the sink, and takes over the first aid duties.

"It turns out I'm a one-pot screamer. Who knew?" he jokes.

She dabs around the deeper cuts, trying to be careful. "You'll need antiseptic on these or they'll get infected. I'll pick some up in the morning."

He winces, feeling the sting. "Great holiday so far."

She sits back, looking angry at the implication that this is her fault. "Who did this, Gray?"

He slowly peels back his shirt from his arm, revealing more damage. "I went for a beer and ran into a couple of local heroes. Apparently 'my kind' don't belong in their bar."

"You're not serious?" she says, as she helps him out of his shirt.

He hods up his bloody arm as exhibit A "This look like I'm joking? I nearly ended up as a hood ornament".

"We have to go to the police," Robyn states flatly. "You could have been killed".

He shakes his head. "They play rough, but I doubt they're homicidal. I just want to forget it happened and go to bed". He can see by her expression that she's unconvinced "What will it achieve, Rob? Let it go."

Robyn silently finishes cleaning up his wounds and hands him the bloody towel. "This will have to do until tomorrow". She takes his hand and leads him back to bed, switching off the bathroom light on the way.

Gray carefully, painfully, crawls between the sheets and flops his head onto the pillow. He stares up at the ceiling. "There was an old Aboriginal woman in the garden bar tonight."

Robyn crawls into bed beside him and quietly waits for him to continue his story.

"Not white, not black, she called me the nowhere man" he sleepily murmurs. "She said that Namarrkon is coming for me" He slurs the words as his eye lids droop and sleep takes him.

"Namarrkon? What is that?" she asks, and waits for an answer that doesn't come. She switches off the bedside light and looks up at the ceiling with the name repeating in her brain. It takes a while, but sleep finally comes and Namarrakon is forgotten for now.

CHAPTER 21

HOPKINS POWER SLIDES THE TOYOTA around the corner, almost losing control. He fishtails up the road and pulls into his driveway. He hits the brakes and pulls up just shy of ramming the house.

Scotty clings onto the roll bar for dear life. "You're fuckin' crazy, mate. Next time, I'm drivin".

Hopkins spills out of the driver's seat and flops onto a well-worn deckchair. "You couldn't drive a greasy stick up a dead dingo's arse". He holds up his hand to signal he's in need of the nectar of the gods.

Scotty reaches over to the back seat, grabs two VB cans. "Incoming," he yells, and tosses one to Hopkins, who catches it on the fly, rips back the ring pull, and covers the eruption of amber fluid with his mouth.

Scotty cracks the tab on his can. "Did you see the look on that fucker's face?"

Hopkins raises his pretend rifle and looks down the sights. "Like a fuckin' Roo frozen in the spotty. Boom." He skulls back the rest of his beer in one hit. "My old man called it right, keep 'em under the fucking boot."

Scotty takes a long chug of his beer, trying to keep up, but he's already pretty pissed and barely holding his shit together.

Hopkins tosses aside the empty and holds his hand out for another. "Dead one".

Scotty grabs a fresh beer. "Live one," and tosses him the replacement. He is genuinely impressed at the man's capacity to handle his grog.

Outwardly, Hopkins seems fine, but inside his thoughts are becoming erratic, with twisted emotions driving deeper into his dark past. Hopkins laments. "They burned him alive. He fought in a war to keep his country free, only to see it invaded straight after" He pops the tab on the can and takes a drink. "You know there wasn't a viewing. Nothing to see here, move along". He stares out into the darkness and shudders at the memory of his father's charred body in the morgue. "But I saw. Oh, yeah, he made bloody sure I saw".

Scotty finishes his beer and stretches out in the seat. "That won't happen here, not here. We're fuckin' kings here, mate".

Hopkins raises his can in a salute and takes another drink "Long live the king". They drink in silence, until Hopkins locks onto another train of thought.

"Roy Marrika, he built them houses, a hospital, a school, out at Yirrikala".

Scotty's eyes are closing, and he sleepily replies, "That's good though, right?"

"Fuck off," barks Hopkins. "They gutted the houses and used the flooring for campfires. You can't domesticate these fucking animals". He skulls the rest of his beer and stares, bleary eyed, at Scotty. "The Abos" he laughs. "The caretakers of the land, they call themselves. They use it as a bargaining chip to fill their grubby pockets". He hurls the empty can into the darkness. "Tasmania was just a fucking good start".

Scotty's eyes close and he drifts into a drunken slumber, but this doesn't stop Hopkins. "They should've kept going until they pushed every last one of them into the Arafura Sea". He bitterly spits out the words. The soft resonating snore is a dead giveaway that he has lost his audience. He staggers to his feet, grabs a dusty blanket from the back of the Toyota, and covers Scotty with it. "Fucking lightweight" he mumbles.

While he's up he grabs another beer, reaches for the ring tab, and freezes, hearing Sarah and Alison's laughter coming from the darkness. He glances towards the swing set and clocks the motionless swings. Tears well in his eyes and he angrily wipes them away. "The fuckers take everything" he whispers.

He cracks the beer and skulls half of it, before sitting back in the deckchair and settling in. "You're not taking anything else from me" he yells into the darkness. "I'll burn it all down first".

？

CHAPTER 22

SENIOR CONSTABLE PATTERSON SCRIBBLES in his notebook as Robyn, the receptionist, and the barman, relay their stories from last night's incident in the bar. "I really need to speak to your husband, and he needs to make a formal complaint," the police officer says to Robyn.

"He says they were just pissed; he doesn't want to pursue it," she replies.

Patterson closes his notebook and pockets it. "Then there isn't much I can do. I'll follow it up as a civil disorder complaint".

The barman and receptionist excuse themselves and go back to work, leaving Robyn and Patterson. "I know Hopkins pretty well, and I'm only too happy to climb up his arse, but it won't go far without your husband's official complaint". Frustration is written all over Robyn's face.

"I shouldn't be telling you this, but this isn't a first for Hopkins. He's a powder keg with a short fuse."

Robyn can't understand how someone like this is not already behind bars, but stops just shy of asking. "Thank you for coming," she says, and then cuts back through the hotel and jogs down to the beach to meet Gray.

The picture-postcard beach stretches as far as the eye can see, and the crystal-clear blue waters gently lap the golden sand. Gray and Robyn walk for hours, until they spot East Woody Island. It's low tide and the sandbar across to the Island is above water, so they cross, hand in hand. They climb over the centre and jump across the rocks.

It's slow going for Gray, with the injuries he's carrying, but they eventually arrive at the ocean side of the island, where they discover a young Indigenous tribesman spear-fishing off the rocks. A movement in the water, a flash of silver, catches his eye. He drives the spear downward and then hauls it back with a good-sized thrashing trevally impaled through the gills.

A young Indigenous girl hurries over and takes the catch from him, then returns to the shade of a large tree. She wraps the fish in palm leaves and adds it to a pile caught earlier. The rest of the mob, around twenty in all, sit in the shade and chat quietly. They look up and spot Gray and Robyn. One of the older women smiles and waves to them.

Robyn and Gray wave back, feeling a like unannounced visitors. The older woman turns to the young girl and quietly speaks to her. The young girl picks up the freshest fish and hurries across the rocks to them. "For you, pretty lady," she says in broken English.

The spear-fisherman waves his spear in the air and yells out to the young girl in his native tongue "Tell him to catch his own fish".

Gray asks the girl, "What did he say?" She smiles and replies, "He said he's happy to share his tucker with you." She thrusts the fish into Gray's hands and quickly scampers back across the rocks to the others. Robyn waves to them. "Thank you!" she calls out. The old woman gives her an offhand wave, as if to say, it's nothing, and goes back to chatting with her family.

Robyn yells to Gray, "Back in minute," and crosses over the rocks to the Indigenous women, leaving Gray to hold the fish and wonder what she's up to. He watches Robyn crouch down and talk to the older woman. The conversation is brief but animated; the woman points to the sky. Robyn takes the woman's hand in hers before rock-hopping back to Gray. "What was that about?" he asks. "I just wanted to thank her properly," replies Robyn. "She said we should cross now, before the tide comes in." She heads back the way they came; Gray waves his thanks to the fisherman once more and the man just shakes his head. "Happy to share, my arse" mutters Gray before following Robyn.

They head back along the beach towards town and she casually drops in, "I spoke to the police this morning," catching Gray off guard. "You did what?".

Robyn is quick to add, "He made it very clear that he couldn't do much without a formal complaint from you".

Gray snaps at her "I told you to let it go".

They walk on in stony silence for a long stretch.

"I don't understand you," she finally says.

He stops and turns angrily towards her. "Why, because I see no point in fighting every battle?" The scornful look she gives him, and her next words rock him to his core.

"Fighting one would be a good start." The moment she says it she feels regret. "Gray..." She wants to take it back, but he cuts her off before she can get the words out.

"Fuck you, Rob" He turns his back on her and strides away. He hears the frustration and anger in her voice, as she yells at his retreating back: "You'll stand up for your clients, but I guess that's because you're getting paid".
⍰

CHAPTER 23

ROBYN HURRIES ALONG THE HOTEL CORRIDOR trying to catch up to him. "Gray, wait up. This is childish. We have to talk" She grabs his arm and he angrily pivots to face her. "Take your hands off me".

She takes a defensive step back, fearful, and instantly sees his eyes fill with shame. She seizes the moment. "I just want you to stand up for yourself and not let this arsehole get away with it".

Gray laughs, but it is cold and humourless. "You mean, stand up for you. Isn't that what this is really about?"

She is genuinely confused. "What the hell is that supposed to mean?"

He looks her straight in the eyes, unwavering. "My path became your journey, and it's a shit-load harder than you thought it was gonna be".

Her anger returns at the accusation. "No, that's not true. I knew exactly..." He cuts her off again and continues unabated. "If they've got no respect for that black fella, imagine what they must think of his fucking white missus, hey? That bitch got bush fever".

She is furious and lashes out at his face with an open hand. The sound of the slap echoes along the corridor.

"And you think I behave like child" He quips.

She fires back without hesitation "No, I think you behave like a coward". Her words hit him harder than anything she could have physically done and in that moment he is prepared to tell her to get out of his life.

The door to a room across from them cracks open, and the sleepy face of an older gent appears in the gap. "Do you mind, we're trying to have a nap in here".

Robyn turns towards the man. "I'm sorry, we'll keep it down" She apologises.

The older gent looks at Gray and whispers to Robyn, "Do you want me to call the police, miss?"

Robyn switches from apologetic to pissed off in the blink of an eye. "Oh fuck off, mate," she snaps.

"You try to help. Some people …" he says, and quickly closes the door.

She turns back to find the corridor empty and Gray nowhere in sight.

CHAPTER 24

ACCORDING TO THE TOWN CLOCK – a three-metre aggregate concrete monolith – the time is 1.15a.m. The town centre is deserted and deathly silent. Four young Indigenous girls wander quietly past the clock and along the path beside the Post Office. They're heading for the town beach, where the rest of their mob are camped for the night.

Hopkins' Toyota slowly cruises along the road and pulls up beside the girls. He leans out of the window and does a quick scan of the area to make sure there are no prying eyes.

One of the girls, Ruby, dressed in a dirty summer frock and nothing else, slinks over and leans against the driver's side door. "Hey, Hopkins, you out late," she purrs.

His gaze drops to her partially exposed breasts, and he feels his cock stir. "Too hot to sleep, Rubes, and the bloody air-con's on the blink."

She licks her lips and inquires. "You got anything to drink?"

He nods. "There's a six pack in the fridge. You wanna send your sisters home and we can go get a cold one?"

She leans in closer and whispers into his ear. "You make it a whole carton this time I fuck you good, better than last time."

He leans away from her and pops open the passenger side door. "Fair enough. Might even toss in a pack of smokes if you do".

Ruby hurries back to the other girls and quickly chatters to them. They hug and then head off down the street without her. She hurries around to the passenger side and climbs in.

Hopkins scans the street again; he doesn't need nor want the opinions of any of the self-righteous fuckers. "Keep your head down and stay out of sight until we get to my place," he orders.

Ruby does as she's told, leans over, unzips his fly and swallows his cock up to his balls.

Hopkins groans with pleasure, drops the clutch, and bunny hops as he drives away. He passes the three giggling girls as he takes the corner and disappears from sight.

Hopkins jackhammers his cock into Ruby. It's more like punishment than making love. She moans loudly and pushes up to meet his angry thrusts, but her thoughts aren't on him or what he's doing to her. Her thoughts are on the prize, the carton of beer and packet of cigarettes. He cums loudly and drives harder, pushing her head against the wall. He pulls out and climbs off the bed, buck naked. No thanks, no praise "Grog's on the table".

Ruby scampers to her knees and grabs his softening cock. "Don't have to go yet ..." She really wants that pack of cigarettes.

He absently slaps her hand aside and glares at her "Don't let the door hit you on the arse on the way out".

Ruby, pouting, slides off the bed, deftly slips the frock over her head, and moves past him into the lounge room Lit only with streaks of light through the window from a streetlamp.

Hopkins, still naked, watches Ruby from the bedroom door as she picks up the carton and searches the table for the promised packet of smokes. "I said, if you were good".

Her teeth flash white as she smiles. "I fuck you real good. You cum bloody hard."

Hopkins laughs cruelly. "I've had better wanks. Now take the piss, before I change my mind."

Ruby protectively slings the carton under her arm. "You drive me back to town to my sisters?"

He mulls it over. "Yeah, I could do that. It'll cost you that carton, though".

She slouches over to the door and opens it a crack, before looking back at him over her shoulder. "Bloody white bastard," she spits, before hurrying out and slamming the door behind her.

Hopkins laughs again. "Bloody white bastard," he says to himself. He catches sight of his father's photograph on the sideboard. A sob catches in his throat and he chokes it back. Rage and self-disgust hit him all at once. "Bloody white bastard." He punches the door over and over again. "Bloody black cunt" he screams. The wood splinters beneath his bruised, bloody knuckles.

Hopkins slams through the bathroom door, steps into the shower, and turns the water up as hot as it will go. Steam quickly fills the bathroom as he scrubs himself raw, paying particular attention to his genitals. Blood flows from a series of minor cuts across the knuckles of his hand, mingling with the water, swirling down the drain, the red contrasting with the white shower base.

His thoughts drift back to his childhood, and the birthday cake his mother always made from scratch. It was a white angel cake with red current jam between the layers, and she would say the same words every year.

He articulates the words quietly to himself: "An angel cake for my angel from heaven".

CHAPTER 25

JUNE 22ND, 1949, HACKNEY, UK.

THE WHITE FLESH PARTS and thick blood-red jam flows from the cut as Hopkins mother slices wedges of Angel cake and plates them for the guests. Not much of a party, Hopkins thinks sulkily to himself, as he watches the cake being placed on each of the plates. He doesn't dare voice this opinion out loud, or he'd cop a fair beating from his father. Sure, there were presents and angel cake, but almost all the guests were his father's boring friends, and all they ever speak about is politics, and how immigration will be the downfall of the Empire.

He's just turned fourteen. At this age you'd think he'd be able to invite his own friends to his party. They could talk about things that were important to them, like marbles, conkers, or which girls' they'd touched in naughty places behind the bike shed. The latter would always bring out the lies. Life is bitterly unfair, he silently laments.

The day thankfully draws to a close and his mother stands sentry while he bathes in the lukewarm water his father has left after taking his bath first. He dresses in his Pyjamas and his mother sends him down to say goodnight to his father. He trots down the stairs and approaches his father's chair from behind. "Damn them!" shouts his father.

Hopkins freezes as he spots a half-empty bottle of gin on the floor beside the chair and realizes that his father is drunk. On the television, a ship, the Windrush, has moored at Tilbury Dock, and thousands of Jamaican immigrants are pouring ashore.

Hopkins' father downs the remains of his drink. "Bleeding race traitors, the lot of them" he mumbles. "Like locusts. They'll strip this country, you mark my words". He searches for the gin and spots Hopkins in the shadows. "How long have you been there?"

Hopkins stammers over his reply "Not long, sir. I've just come to say goodnight".

His father refills his glass and then motions for him to come closer.

Hopkins approaches cautiously, all too familiar with his father's unpredictable temper. He stops at the side of the chair and quietly waits to be spoken to.

His father's focus is back on the screen. "See this? They'll be diluting the bloodline before we know it" he says. "Someone has to stand up and say, enough" It comes out sounding like a war cry.

Hopkins holds out his hand to shake his father's. There are no kisses in this family. "Goodnight, Father" he whispers timidly.

His father ignores him, picks up the phone, and dials a local number. "Are you watching the news?" he asks the person on the other end of the line. "I know. Something has to be done".

Hopkins backs away towards the stairs, and the last thing he hears is "Meet me at my shop tomorrow morning. It's time we had a chat". He turns and scampers up the stairs to bed where he can turn his thoughts to important matters like the girls behind the bike shed and what he'd do next time if the chance arose.
⍰

CHAPTER 26

MARCH, 1960, HACKNEY, UK

THE WHITE DEFENCE LEAGUE reads the sign above store. In the window are racist propaganda leaflets, a handful of Bibles, and a lone copy of Mein Kampf.

A news camera crew has set up on the pavement and the reporter is interviewing Hopkins' father. "On the contrary," he says to the interviewer, "the trouble was here long before we set up our headquarters in this area".

A small group of curious locals have gathered. Hopkins nudges his way through with his new girlfriend on his arm. There have been lots of girls over the years, but he's twenty-five now and ready to settle down. Besides, he's nuts over Sharon, and so absolutely sure she's the one that he's brought her to meet the old man.

His father clocks Hopkins with a big-titted bird on his arm and nearly flubs his well-prepared speech. He stumbles over a couple of words, but seamlessly picks it up again. "The fact is that until now, the people haven't had a political outlet for their indignation at the evils of the coloured invasion. Instead, they've resorted to violence. We now offer them a constitutional political outlet. And we therefore think our presence in this area militates against violence, rather than for it".

He patiently waits for the follow-up question, and takes the opportunity to check out Sharon's tits again. Her eyes are on the sign above the shop, and her mouth is open. She lowers her gaze and catches him blatantly checking her out.

The interviewer clears his throat and fires off the next loaded question "What do you consider are the dangers of an increasing coloured population?"

Hopkins father doesn't bat an eyelid and replies, "Well, there are many immediate evils of such an invasion, well known to everybody living in this area – the long-term one, of mass interbreeding ..."

Hopkins studies the faces of the people in the audience, and is surprised to see two black men arrive. His train of thought is savagely interrupted by Sharon's elbow in his ribs. "Jesus, babe," he says, "What the fuck was that for?"

Her eyes are brimming with tears. "I'm leaving. You can stay, but I'm going with or without you".

Hopkins holds her gently and tries to reason with her. "But, babe, you haven't met me olds yet".

She pulls away from his grip, "And I don't want to!" she spits, with venom in her tone.

He glances towards his father, and then back at her. He'd heard others condemn his fathers ideology and wasn't ignorant to the fact that it was extreme, but he had never been put in a position of having to make a choice.

"Well, are you coming?" she asks.

In that instant, he chooses her over his father, light over darkness. She takes his hand and they push through the crowd with his father's voice still droning on behind them: "We feel you cannot have coloured immigration on this scale without, sooner or later, having mass interbreeding. That must lead, ultimately, to a mixed-race Britain. In so far as we believe the civilization and culture of our country is the product of our race, we feel that if we have a mixed-race population in the future, that must mean the downfall of the civilization and the culture of our country which we hold so dear".

Hopkins and Sharon round the corner and run up the street, hand in hand, blinded by infatuation. He often wonders, when looking back on that day – would he have done anything differently, had he known that was the last time he'd see his father alive?

That night, two men in balaclavas hurled Molotov cocktails through the window of the White Defence League.

The place went up in a fireball that could have taken out the block, had it not been for the quick actions of the local fire brigade. It was only later that they found out his father had been working late and was inside when the attack took place.

The following day, Hopkins follows his uncle into the morgue with an aging mortuary attendant, who leads them into a room with row upon row of empty surgical tables - empty except for one.

The attendant flicks a switch and the lights slowly flicker into life. They are led to a table where a body lies beneath a sheet. The attendant looks at Hopkins' uncle – Are you sure?

His uncle nods his head. The sheet is pulled back and Hopkins comes face to face with the charred remains of his father. He looks away, repulsed, but his uncle forces him to turn back. "You need to see this" he says. "This is what they do".

Hopkins looks at the eyes; they can't be closed because the eyelids have been seared off. The pupils are milky-white. He literally thinks he will go insane. A silent scream rips up from deep inside him.

Of course, the papers had a field day with the story, and he and his mother were hounded for months, but it all eventually died down and the press moved on to something more interesting. But the harassment from a local coloured group never ended. They wanted Hopkins and his family to know that they were always watching.

By this stage, Hopkins and Sharon were well into their relationship, after he had convinced her that his father's ideology had not taken root in him.

No more than six months after the fire, Hopkins' uncle was stabbed to death on his way home from the pub. Nobody was ever tied to the crime, but Hopkins knew who it was. Around the same time, Hopkins' mother was handed a death sentence in the form of a breast cancer diagnosis. "This family is cursed," she said to Hopkins and Sharon, after delivering the news. The same day she sold her home, cleaned out her bank account, and handed almost all of it over to her son with one proviso "Leave this godforsaken country and never come back. They'll be coming for you next".

Sharon was ecstatic when Hopkins proposed the move to her. "A fresh start!" she chirped. "Where should we go?"

"What do you think about year-round sunshine, beaches that stretch as far as the eye can see, and wildlife that comes right up to your backdoor?"

She'd beamed at the thought. "I think it sounds like paradise. Where is this place?"

"Australia" he'd grandly declared.

They departed from London in late 1960, arriving in Sydney soon after. Sharon got a production line job, and Hopkins found work in a chemical plant. They were doing pretty well and bought house in Parramatta, but city life wasn't what Hopkins was looking for, and a chance comment by a workmate put him onto a company looking for employees in the Northern Territory.

Sharon took some convincing when she found out that anything and everything that could kill you lived in the Territory, nine of the deadliest variety of snakes in the world, droughts, venomous spiders, floods, salt water crocodiles, Jelly fish, and sharks. But she finally relented when he promised that they could come back to Sydney if it didn't work out.

In mid 1961 they drove out of Sydney, cut through the dead centre of Australia, and became Territorians – at least, he did. Sharon never really took to life in a mining town, and would have left had their first girl not come along in '66. Even then, Sharon battled with depression and it eventually soured their relationship.

They had their second girl in '69, in an attempt to bring them closer together, but Hopkins was already fucking everything he could lay his hands on, and the rest of his time was split between work, the pub, and hunting with his mates.

Sharon frequently asked herself what she had done wrong to make him act like this, but the truth was that the dye had been cast long before, and the real nature of the man had simply risen to the surface.

？

CHAPTER 27

"WHERE ARE YOU OFF TO?" Gray looks up from packing camping gear into the back of the four-wheel drive and into the smiling face of the same receptionist who'd booked them in on their arrival. "Camping in the wilds," he answers.

Robyn joins them, carrying a couple of shopping bags full of food. "The Goyder River. Am I saying it right?" she asks.

"Any better, I'd think you were a Territorian," replies the receptionist. "Just be careful out there. It's a long way back to town if anything goes wrong."

Robyn passes the shopping bags to Gray and he cushions them between the sleeping bag and the tent. Neither speaks or looks at the other; things are still icy between them.

Robyn gives the receptionist a hug. "We'll be fine. See you in a couple of days."

Gray closes up the back and they climb into the vehicle. The receptionist speaks to Gray through the driver's side window. "Listen, about what happened in the bar the other night. I just want you to know, we're not all like that up here".

He smiles for the first time that morning "I know".

The receptionist leans through the window and turns on the CB radio mounted above the dash. The call sign is taped to the unit. "Keep it on. You never know" she advises him.

Gray replies with a salute. "Will do." He starts the vehicle, slips the clutch, and pulls away.

"Oh, hey," yells the receptionist.

Gray slams on the brakes and pokes his head out of the window.

"Merry Christmas, for tomorrow" she calls out.

Gray and Robyn respond in kind. "Merry Christmas to you too" Although it had completely slipped their minds, with everything else going on between them. They drive the short distance to the petrol station, where Gray tops up the tank and fills a couple of additional jerry cans for safety's sake. A great survival tip from his father: never get caught in the bush without food, water or fuel.

"Do you want anything?" asks Robyn.

He shakes his head and replies flatly. "No".

Robyn heads inside to pay, disappearing from his sight on the far side of the vehicle. She enters the shop and stands behind a customer who is paying the attendant for his fuel.

A man, wearing a baseball cap, searches through a rack loaded with fan belts and radiator hoses. He has his back to the counter.

There's a dusty old AWA radio mounted on a shelf in the corner. The announcer's voice sounds tinny through the mono-speaker. "It's the twenty-third of December and the time is seven forty-five in the A.M. Tropical Cyclone Tracy is currently situated two hundred and ten kilometres west-north-west of Darwin and is moving south at four kilometres per hour. The centre is expected to be ..." The attendant spins the tuning dial and changes the channel to a music station.

"Think we'll cop any of that?" asks the customer.

"Nah, reckon she'll slide right past, same as Selma and the one before that, and before that" replies the attendant as he hands him his change.

The customer exits and Robyn steps up to the counter. "We're heading out to the Goyder River today" she says. "Are you sure?"

"Yeah, it's tracking away from Darwin" Says the Attendant. "I reckon the most we'll get might be a bit of a blow job" he adds with a salacious grin.

"Well, there's a first time for everything" Robyn says sweetly.

The smile slides from the attendant's face "Thirty-two, seventy-five".

Robyn pays him, takes her change, and leaves the shop.

The man wearing the baseball cap turns to the attendant and drops a radiator belt onto the counter. It is Scotty, and he follows Robyn out with his eyes, partially hidden beneath the peak of his cap. His gaze is locked onto her arse.

Gray steps out from behind the vehicle with a jerry can in each hand and loads them into the rear. Scotty recognizes him and quickly turns away before he's recognised. "You've gotta be shittin' me" he whispers to himself. A wolfish grin spreads across his face.
⍰

CHAPTER 28

THE STORM

DECEMBER 24TH, 1974.

JOSEPH TOSSES MORE IRONBARK LEAVES into the fire
pit he's dug into the sand. The buffeting winds have
made it necessary to dig deep, or it simply gets blown
away. The sky above is a broiling mass of green-tinged
clouds. "Namarrkon, I was born on this Island, you know
me, my name is Joseph," he calls out to the storm as he
wafts the swirling smoke over his face and into the air,
where it is instantly snatched away by the shrieking
wind. "This is my land, the land of my people".

The trees lining the beach are bent over under the
onslaught of the storm, and one snaps with a sound like
a gunshot. The gust hits Joseph, driving him off his feet,
tumbling him across the sand towards the water's edge.

"Grandfather!" His granddaughter and her husband
fight the wind to come to his aid. They help him regain
his feet, just as the sky lights up and a lightning bolt
strikes the water with a deafening crack. "We have to
get to the mission with the others," yells his
granddaughter.

Joseph hesitates. He wants to stay and plead longer with Namarrkon, but the storm god's fury is great and he seems not to be listening. Joseph looks at his granddaughter's face and sees the fear in her eyes. "Alright, granddaughter," he yells.

The three of them huddle together and stagger through the raging storm towards the safety of the mission.

Tracy brushes past the Tiwi Islands; homes and businesses are damaged by the gale-force winds, but not a single life is lost, and the Mission is miraculously left untouched.

Everyone taking shelter within the mission thank the white God for his divine blessing, but not Joseph – he thanks Namarrkon for listening to his story and sparing his people.
?

CHAPTER 29

GRAY PULLS OFF THE SEALED ROAD and stops beside a weather-ravaged sign reads: GOYDER RIVER 180 KMS. Beyond the sign is the rough-as-guts, muddy, dirt track. He gets out and locks the wheels hubs.

Robyn gets out with a camera and takes a picture of the sign, the start of the track, and Gray crouched down by the rear wheel. "Hey" she calls out to him. He glances up at her and she does a really weird-looking motion with the fingers and thumbs of one hand.

"What, Rob, I have no idea what that is" he says confused and irritated.

She keeps making contorted finger movements "It's sign language-ish. It's either this or we just don't communicate with each other the entire time we're out here".

He locks in the final hub and stands to face her. "What else is there to say? You made yourself pretty bloody clear".

"I was angry, and I let my emotions get the better of me. I said some things that I didn't mean". She goes to him and gently kisses his cheek "From the bottom of my heart, I'm sorry". She gently kisses his lips "Forgive me?"

He takes a moment before kissing her back "Forgiven".

She takes a step back and does her sign language-ish thing again.

"What the hell does that mean?" he asks, laughing.

She points along the track "We gotta go that-a-way.

That-a-way-ish? He replies.

Robyn grins "Just follow the sign".

They climb back into the vehicle and set off along the track. Hours later they are manoeuvring through a muddy river bed, and narrowly miss a drift of wild pigs that bursts out from the underbrush ahead of them. Gray slams on the brakes and they skid to a shuddering halt. There's a large wallow at the side of the track, filled with churned up mud, where the pigs have been cooling themselves.

"Oh my god." Robyn fumbles for her camera "Look at the size of him". She snaps off a half-dozen quick shots. The huge boar with six-inch tusks stands its ground while the rest of the pack escapes into the surrounding scrub.

"Looks like Porky Pig's been hitting the gym," Gray says in awe.

The boar stares fearlessly back at them, before turning away and trotting after the drift.

"I wonder what they eat?" Robyn asks.

"Anything they bloody well want" Gray replies, as he slips the clutch and continues driving along the muddy track towards the river.
?

CHAPTER 30

THE GLOWING CIGARETTE BUTT spirals down towards the two police officers as they exit the worksite with the shift supervisor in tow. Hopkins is on the catwalk high above, willing the smoking projectile to find its target. Behind him, a crew of sweaty labourers haul loads of bricks across scaffolding planks into a huge kiln flanked by two others. They designed to dry the cake, producing the white aluminium powder the plant was built for. The heat coming off the kilns is stifling and the noise deafening. Everyone working on site is wearing boots, a hard hat, safety goggles, and a noise-reduction headset.

Scotty climbs up the last of the stairs and spots Hopkins leaning against the safety rail. Both men slip their hearing protection up onto their helmets.

"What did those fuckwits want?" Scotty yells.

"The Abo from the bar the other night," Hopkins yells back. "Apparently he didn't think we were very hospitable to him. I'm done. Two weeks notice and I'm being flown out".

"Fuck, mate, that's bullshit" Scotty lights up two smokes and hands one to Hopkins. "I saw him and his missus at the servo this morning." Hopkins appears mildly interested.

"She's got a primo set of tits, nice arse" Scotty contours her outline in the air with his hands.

"You mean, not bad for a gin, right?" asks Hopkins.

Scotty slowly shakes his head and grins like the Cheshire cat, drawing out the telling. "Nah, mate".

Hopkins has already had a shit morning and his patience is quickly wearing thin. "I've got work to do. Fuck off," he yells.

Scotty's smile falters. "You know, sometime you just suck the joy out of life".

Hopkins slips his hearing protection over his ears and signs to Scotty that he can't hear him.

Scotty yells into his face: "She's white".

Hopkins looks into his eyes for a long moment to gauge if he's taking the piss.

"As the driven' fuckin' snow, mate" continues Scotty.

Hopkins takes a drag of his cigarette and processes this information as he blows a steady stream of smoke into the air. "A white gin" he says to himself.

Scotty knows he's got the floor again and plays out the moment. "That's not all, but I know you're busy, so I'll …"

Hopkins flicks his cigarette butt at his face and narrowly misses. "Alright, fuckin' hell – they're camping out at the Goyder".

Hopkins grins. "You're definite? They're heading for the Goyder?"

Scotty nods his head emphatically.

"Get hold of Wilksy and Johannson – we're going on one last fishing trip".

Scotty takes a drag of his smoke. "Johannson, really?"

Hopkins shrugs. "The fat prick grows the best ganja on the peninsula".

Scotty can't argue with that logic, free ganja. He flicks his cigarette butt over the rail and scurries away to tell the others.

Hopkins turns back to the safety rail and looks out over the plant site, already beginning to justify the actions he's about to set in motion. The Abo started that shit in the bar, just by being there. He got off light.

Now he's brought the cops to Hopkins' workplace and cost him his job. Not for a moment does he question why he isn't in a cell already. That would mean taking into consideration that no charges had been officially laid. Then there would be no reason for the righteous anger growing inside him.

He turns away from reason and focuses on the grim possibilities. No job, no residency permit – without a permit he's driven out of his home. No, the Abo came into his world, he started this shit, so it's only fair that he returns the favour, nothing too serious, just a bit of harmless fun. But the cold, dark look in his eyes is in stark contrast to his thoughts.

？

CHAPTER 31

GRAY LOCKS UP THE BRAKES and Robyn quickly jumps out, camera already in her hand. In the distance, an enormous female water buffalo with horns at least four feet wide lumbers through the wet plain. "Look at it. It's amazing," she whispers, as she clicks off shot after shot.

Gray joins her, hanging back out of her line of sight. "Imagine the size of the steaks," he says quietly.

She turns to him with a look of mock horror. "You wouldn't?"

A calf trots over to join the Female and Gray is instantly captivated. "Rob," he whispers, and points it out.

She turns back and her heart melts. "Oh, my, God. So beautiful." She raises the camera and quickly focuses. Click! Click! Click!

They drive on for another half a kilometre, and reach the Goyder River crossing. Gray pulls off the track and parks on a flat area, a safe distance from the riverbank. They climb out of the vehicle and take in the surrounding landscape. Recent rainfall has the river level up, but not impassable, as it can apparently sometimes become.

Deep grooves mark either side of the river crossing, where four-wheel-drive vehicles have previously clawed their way up the banks. On either side of these markings are slide paths. Gray points them out to Robyn. "From crocs sliding down the bank". Now it's his turn to laugh as a worried look crosses her face. "It's okay," he reassures her. "We'll set the tent well back from the river and build a big fire".

Gray hammers in the last of the tent pegs and steps back to survey his handiwork, as Robyn staggers out of the bush with a load of firewood stacked up to her chin. She dumps it in the clearing. "This stuff isn't light, buddy".

He beats his chest. "Fire, food, shelter – I am a hunter-gather."

"Come on, Tarzan. We need a lot more firewood than this," she says over her shoulder as she heads back into the surrounding bush.

"But baby, I put up the tent," he calls out to her retreating back.

Her voice drifts back. "And I may even let you sleep in it, if you behave".

He promptly follows her into the bush, in case she's serious. "Harsh, Rob, very harsh".

The most amazing sunset colours the sky a vivid red and casts a warm glow over the river. Jabiru and magpie geese search the riverbank and shallows for their evening meals.

Gray and Robyn sit with their backs against a log in front of a roaring fire, presiding over paradise. He pokes the dancing flames with a long branch. "You know, we should have gone in search of my roots in Mauritius – nice five-star hotel, swimming pool, and a cocktail bar" he says out of the blue.

"Okay, I'll bite" she says after a moment.

"It's an island two thousand kilometres off the south-eastern coast of Africa" he replies.

She nudges him hard. "I know where Mauritius is, but why would we be going there?" she asks.

"Well, if you ask any kid from St Kilda Primary where I come from, they'll tell you Mauritius". He tosses the stick onto the fire. "You were right, I am a coward".

Robyn puts an arm over his shoulder. "I'm not the one walking in your shoes" She snuggles in close.

He leans away from her embrace. "I lied about where I came from because I was ashamed. I hated Dad for being white and Mum for marrying him.

I spent decades hating the two people who gave me life. They loved me and I blamed them for every beating I took at school, every insult …" Tears begin streaming down his cheeks. "I've spent so long hiding that I don't know who I am anymore".

She fiercely embraces him. "I know who you are" she says softly, and reaches up with one hand to gently turn his face towards hers. Her eyes also brim with tears and the firelight reflects off them. "You're the man I love, that's who you are. You're the father of the child I'm carrying, that's who you are". She gazes into his eyes and waits for her words to sink in.

His mind reels over the revelation of the pregnancy – he's going to be a father, and he is suddenly overwhelmed by a rush of mixed emotions.

"I wanted the news to be your Christmas present" she tells him.

"What if I mess it up?" he asks.

She smiles at him. "We'll both mess up. We'll both learn by our mistakes. I have no doubt you're going to be an amazing father, but our child needs to know where she comes from".

Doubt still clouds his thoughts. "I just don't want him having to fight every day of his life".

"She ..." Robyn corrects him "will no doubt get in her fair share of scraps, but she needs a strong, proud father to guide her when that happens".

Gray understands exactly what she's asking of him. "Did dad know?" he asks.

"The last night you were with him – that wasn't an ottoman he was making. He knew and he kept the secret" she replies.

He takes her in his arms and kisses her eyes, cheeks, and lips. "I love you" he says between kisses.

She responds in kind "I love you too".

He gently places a hand on her belly "When is he due?"

She smiles sweetly and replies "She, will be meeting her daddy in August".

They hold onto each other under a blanket of stars in a world that, right at this moment, belongs to no one else but them.

⍰

CHAPTER 32

THE RECEPTION LIGHTS BUST INTO LIFE as the Walkabout hotel receptionist prepares her workspace for the day ahead. She turns on the radio and listens to the news on a small portable radio as she makes her first heart-starter of the morning. Two teaspoons of instant coffee to give her a jolt. The jug boils and she begins filling her cup. The radio announcer's voice conveys a sense of urgency that immediately captures her attention and stays her hand.

"At six a.m. CST Tropical Cyclone Tracey was centred west, northwest of Darwin and moving south at four KPH. The centre is expected to be one hundred kilometres west of Darwin at six pm today".

Her thoughts go straight to that nice couple camping out at the Goyder river. She puts down the jug, picks up the phone, and dials the number for the local police station.

CHAPTER 32

THE DREAMING

GRAY'S EYES SLOWLY OPEN – something has disturbed his sleep, but he's not sure what. He checks on Robyn; she's still sleeping soundly beside him. He reaches out and gently, so as not to wake her, places his hand on her belly.

The tent flap whips noisily on the breeze; it's probably what woke him in the first place. He makes a move to secure it, and comes face to snout with the bull crocodile as it pushes its head into the tent. The fear he felt on their last encounter is still there, but he forces it down in his belly and reaches out a hand to touch this magnificent creature. As his hand makes contact the wind shrieks and the tent flaps dance around the croc's head.

[?]

CHAPTER 33

GRAY IS JOLTED AWAKE to discover the tent flaps dancing crazily in the wind and the rain coming down in sheets.

Robyn peeks out from her sleeping bag. "Are we okay?"

"It's torrential. We're not going anywhere in this" he replies. "Go back to sleep".

She unzips her sleeping bag and ushers him in. "Come back to bed" He doesn't need to be asked twice and slips in beside her.

The storm passes quickly; Gray slides out of the sleeping bag and slips on his pants. Robyn is still sleeping, so he quietly exits the tent without waking her.

He wanders over to the river for a much-needed piss, and after unzipping, aims the stream into the river. He yawns, stretches, and tries not to piss on his feet. Something large on the far bank, further down the river, catches his eye. He relizes what it is and his bladder freezes mid-stream. He backs away from the water and makes his way back to the tent. He pulls back the flaps, and whispers excitedly, "Rob. Get up".

Robyn mutters from the edge of a deep sleep, "Just ten more minutes".

He tugs at the bottom of her sleeping bag. "Grab your camera and come with me"

She sits up. "What?" But Gray has already disappeared.

Robyn finds Gray at the water's edge looking towards the far bank. "Okay, I'm up. What's so important?"

"Merry Christmas – I got you a handbag" He points further up the river on the opposite bank. "And a pair of boots".

She follows the direction his finger is pointing in, and it takes a moment for her brain to recognize the behemoth she's looking at. A bull crocodile at least five metres from head to tail. Robyn fumbles for her camera and consciously has to steady her hands to set the focus. "Oh, my God, he's huge. The last of the dinosaurs" she says reverently, and clicks off shot after shot.

Gray takes in every detail of the croc, its huge feet, armour-plated hide, massive jaws, that powerful tail. He feels a pull towards the creature, a sense of respect, not just because it could end his life in a heartbeat; it's something more, something he can't quite put his finger on.

He dismisses this fleeting thought as just stupid imagination, certain that an encounter between them would lead to him being excreted as a large heap of steaming croc turd.

⍰

CHAPTER 34

THE PUNGENT SMELL of oily heads and buds fills Johannson's poky room. There is barely enough room for the single bed, desk, and wardrobe currently occupying the space. A couple of Scout recruitment posters hang on the wall, along with photographs of Johannson dressed in his Scout Master's uniform. He's at a jamboree with some of the boys standing by his side. Lying on the bed is a backpack and a hunting rifle.

Johannson shreds the ganja and packs it into a metal tin the size of a child's lunchbox. A second box sits on the desktop with the lid off, its interior crammed full of Polaroids. The top layer of photographs are of young boys, naked or semi-naked. His eyes constantly flick from the task at hand to the photographs. He pauses to pull his cock from his pants, massage the ganja oil into the head and shaft, and focus solely on his beautiful boys.

The sound of approaching footsteps out in the corridor brings him to a shuddering halt. He quickly closes the lid of the box containing the Polaroids, smearing the surface with the oil, and drops it into the bottom left-hand drawer of his desk. The footsteps are getting closer, and the last thing he needs is to get busted with a shitload of weed in his possession.

He crams the rest of the shredded ganja into the tin, drops that into the bottom right-hand desk drawer, sweeps the stems into a plastic bag, bins them, and towels the oil off his hands.

The footsteps stop at Johannson's door as he slides onto his bed and picks up a scouting magazine. There's a rapid knock. He tries' to sound as casual as possible. "It's open," he calls out.

The door swings open to reveal Wilks standing there with a backpack and a rifle slung over his shoulders. "That's a neat trick" says Wilks with a grin.

Johannson doesn't have a clue what he's talking about. "You really are a retard"

"Maybe" says Wilks, "but I'm not the dumb cunt reading a magazine upside down".

Johannson clocks the magazine, and it is indeed upside down. "I was packing the weed and you came – never mind".

The sound of a horn blaring outside makes them both jump. "He's in a mood" Wilks warns him. The horn blares again.

Johannson jumps to his feet, grabs his pack and his rifle, and hurries past Wilks.

He's halfway down the hall before he realizes he's forgotten the ganja. He waves to Wilks, who's just about to close the door to his room, and silently mouths: "Grab the weed – bottom left-hand drawer" Before scurrying along the corridor towards the exit.

Wilk re-enters the room. He looks at the desk, bottom left, and pauses, confused "Left hand drawer" he mutters to himself. The concept of left and right has been an issue with him his entire life. His mother had taught him to wear his watch on his left wrist – if he wanted to know left from right, think of the watch, she'd said.

Wilks' watch had been broken the day before and he hadn't had time to get it repaired yet. Without his watch to guide him, and rushed by the sound of the horn blaring outside, Wilks pulls open the bottom right-hand drawer and plucks out the wrong tin. He lovingly sniffs the pungent oil smeared all over its surface, and rams it into his backpack, before leaving the room.

Hopkins leans on the horn again as Johannson runs toward them with his pack swinging wildly. "You're gonna wake up the night crew" he calls out to Hopkins.

Hopkins stays on the horn a moment longer to piss them all off. "Where's the weed?" he asks.

Johannson points back at the block. "Wilksy's got it".

Hopkins fires up the engine. "Alright, throw your kit in the dinghy and get your fat arse in the back" he orders.

Johannson does as instructed and manoeuvres his bulky frame onto the cramped back seat.

Wilks runs out of the block. "Wait on, ya bloody yobbo" He tosses his pack into the dinghy and squeezes into the little space left on the back seat. "Breathe in, will'ya, mate". Johannson wriggles to the side, but it makes little to no difference.

Scotty hurls himself into the passenger seat as Hopkins floors the accelerator and drops the clutch. The Toyota spears off the mark, leaving dirt, debris, and disgruntled night-shift-workers, in its wake.
⏃

CHAPTER 35

TOWERING ANTHILLS DOMINATE THE LANDSCAPE for miles in every direction. Robyn strolls between them, stopping occasionally as she finds the right frame and snaps off a shot.

Gray stalks her, unseen, watching as she looks for a fresh composition to capture through the lens of her camera.

She follows a trail of ants moving across the surface of the hill carrying sticks and leaves, zooms in, focuses, and snaps off a couple of shots. "Thanks, fellas" she says to the ants.

Gray puts on his best interpretation of an ant's voice. "Hey, lady, what do you call an army of ants?"

She jumps at the sound of his voice and turns to find him leaning against another anthill. "Milit-ant," he says, laughing at his own joke.

Robyn just shakes her head. "That was an anti-climax," she fires back.

Unlike her, he laughs. "Quick, Rob, very quick."

She turns 360 degrees on the spot, taking in everything around her and breathing in the warm, clean air "I'm inspired, Gray, this place ..."

He follows her gaze. "It's magical. Thanks for giving me a shove" He looks less stressed, and the constant scowl he's been wearing has fallen away.

"Don't move, not a muscle" she says, as she brings the camera up and focuses the lens on him. "You're magical" she whispers.

His eyes light up and a smile pushes up the corners of his mouth. Her voice becomes husky. "Take off your shirt".

He doesn't hesitate, slowly undoing one button at a time and slipping his shirt down his arms until it hangs from the waist of his jeans.

Robyn clicks off shot after shot. "Unbutton your jeans" she orders.

"These had better not show up in the post-holiday slide show at your mum's" he jokes.

"Jeans," she growls.

Gray's hand drops to the waist of his jeans and her lens follows.

She focuses on his fingers undoing the fly buttons. "Fuck it". She places the camera on the ground and charges towards him.

Gray catches her in full flight and is driven back against the anthill. She kisses him, and tears at his jeans while he rips off her shorts, their hungry lips not separating for a moment. Gray lifts her up by her hips and she wraps her legs around him. He slides up to the hilt inside her, and she grinds against him. They climax together and his legs give out beneath him.

They sit, perched against the anthill, still wrapped in each other's limbs. "It's gotta be something in the air" he says breathlessly.

She moans, grinds against him, and says "Welcome to the Territory".

He bursts out laughing, and the sound echoes across the landscape.

CHAPTER 36

THE FEMALE WATER BUFFALO'S legs fold beneath her and the shot that ends her life rings out a thousandth of a second later. Her calf bolts on instinct, but quickly stops when he realizes his mother is not with him. The calf meanders back to its mother's body and nuzzles her belly. The bullet that enters his brain, just behind the ear, kills him instantly. The calf slumps against his mother's cooling flesh and his eye glaze over.

Hopkins, confident of the kill, slings his rifle over his shoulder and unsheathes a Bowie knife as he strides across the sodden plain.

Scotty, Wilks and Johannson watch from the safety of the Toyota parked on the track. Johannson's laugh comes out as a snort and his words drip sarcasm. "Jungle Jim, off to save the day".

Scotty glances back at him with clear contempt. "Say it to his face, if you've got the balls?"

Johannson's mouth flaps, but no words come out.

"I didn't think so, no merit badge in it" With that he punches Wilks in the arm. "No merit badge, get it?" he repeats.

Wilks is too intently focused on what Hopkins is doing to give a shit.

Hopkins kneels down beside the calf and hacks the head from the body, displaying little or no emotion in the brutal act. He carries it back to the others and tosses it to Johannson. "Heads up" he calls, only after it's been released and airborne.

Johannson catches it clumsily and ends up spattered in thick red blood. "Oh, flaming hell" he bemoans. "What am I supposed to do with this?"

"Toss it in the dinghy" says Hopkins. He looks at the blood covering Johannson's clothing. "And then get in there with it. You're not getting that shit on my seats".

Johannson's mouth flaps open again. "But you..."

Hopkins cuts him off. "I can leave you out here...".

Johannson knows this is not an idle threat. He tosses the head into the dinghy and sullenly climbs in to join it.

Wilks hasn't moved, and continues to stare at the buffalo carcasses. "Aren't we going to butcher the cow?"

Scotty can't stop grinning. "Ain't buff meat we're after" he says.

Wilks looks to Hopkins. "Tell me you're not poaching bloody crocs?"

Scotty laughs. "Cold and getting colder" he teases.

Hopkins snaps, "Shut up, Scotty".

Scotty's smile slips. "I didn't mean nothin".

Hopkins gives him no quarter. "Then do as you mean, say nothing".

Wilks interjects "I don't need any more trouble, and the rangers …"

Hopkins drops a hand on his shoulder. "There isn't a ranger within cooey of us – besides, you can take my word on it, it's not crocs we're after".

Johannson's eyes flick from the calf's severed head lying at his feet to Hopkins. "Then what are we doing out here?".

Hopkins smiles thinly as he replies, "It's a big fat, fucking, Christmas surprise. Get in".

They load up and drive along the track, Johannson holding on for dear life as he's violently bounced around in the dinghy.

Hopkins veers off the track just under a click before the river crossing and drives further upstream. Within minutes a makeshift corrugated-iron shed, surrounded by car parts comes into view. Hopkins does a U-turn so the dinghy can be easily backed into the river. They all climb out and immediately begin unpacking.

Hopkins, rifle in hand, heads down river. "Keep the noise down, I'll be back soon" he calls back over his shoulder and quickly disappears into the bush.

Wilks glances up as the branches above their heads bow with a sudden gust of wind. Dark clouds fill the sky in the distance. "Green clouds at night, shepherds' delight ..."

Johannson joins him. "It's red clouds at night, shepherd's delight. That's a good sign," he reassures Wilks. "We'll be lucky to see rain".

Wilks isn't so sure. "What's the saying for green clouds?"

Johannson follows his line of sight. The rolling black clouds have moved a lot closer, and the green tinge surrounding them is clearly visible. "Shepherd run like hell" Which is what his intuition is telling him to do right now.
⁇

CHAPTER 37

THE ABO'S HEAD IS DEAD CENTRE of the starlight scope.
Hopkins tracks with him as he carries the dinner dishes
back from the river to join his woman by the campfire.

Hopkins is using the fork of a sapling as a tripod to
stabilize his rifle. "Too easy. Bam! Bam!" he whispers to
himself. The wind suddenly picks up, buffeting him and
sending a surge rippling across the surface of the river.
A flock of birds erupts noisily from the trees, taking to
the air.

The couple look up at the sky and Hopkins follows their
gaze. A massive wall of black and green storm clouds is
rolling towards them. He checks his watch – it's just
gone twenty-hundred hours. He takes another look
through the scope. "Storm's coming" he whispers. He
slings his rifle and hurries back the way he came.

"Namarrkon" Robyn says, as they watch lightning
spiderweb across the storm front. The wind picks up
and the trees sway under its force.

Gray glances questioningly at her "What does it mean?"
he asks.

"Remember the woman who gave us the fish?" He nods,
yes. "She told me that Namarrkon is the storm god".

An alarm goes off in Gray's head. Namarrkon is coming for you. He scrambles to his feet. "We haven't checked in since we got here".

They hurry over to the vehicle, and Gray switches the CB radio on. He lifts the hand-piece from its cradle and depresses the send button. "Gove base. Gove base. This is Sierra, Whiskey, two – Over".

The CB crackles with static. "Sierra, whiskey, two, this is Gove Base. Over".

"Gove Base, what's the weather situation? Over".

The soft pitter-patter of rain hits the windscreen.

"What's your position? Over".

"We're still at the Goyder River crossing. There's a storm heading our way. Should we dig in here and ride it out? Over".

There's a short pause before the measured response "Negative. Suggest you pack up immediately and head back into town as fast and as safely as you can. We have a category four cyclone heading for us. Over".

The gravity of the situation is not lost on either of them. "Understood. Moving out now. Sierra, whiskey, two. Out".

Gray replaces the CB's hand-piece. "Pack the sleeping bags and I'll strike the tent" he says with quiet urgency. The rain increases from a drizzle to a downpour in the blink of an eye. Gray grabs a couple of raincoats from a bag on the back seat and tosses one to Robyn.

"Have we got enough time?" she asks in concern.

"We'll be fine," he promises. "But we have to move quickly". They pull on the raincoats and begin the task of breaking camp in the midst of a torrential downpour and howling winds.

Gray tosses the last of their equipment into the back of the vehicle, races around to the driver's door, and scrambles in to join Robyn, who's already in the passenger seat. He starts the engine, turns on the lights and the windscreen wipers. The wiper blades sweep the rain away and Robyn gasps in shock. Two men are revealed, dressed in saturated ponchos, with rifles aimed at the vehicle.

One of the men commands loudly "Out! Now!"

Gray recognizes him immediately – Hopkins "Jesus Christ!"

Hopkins yells the command again "I won't tell you again".

"Get down" Gray tells Robyn, and then flattens the accelerator and drops the clutch.

Hopkins fires a shot into the front tyre, instantly deflating it, and shredding the tyre wall.

The vehicle slews to one side and stalls. Gray tries to restart it "Come on!" But another round fired above them stays his hand.

Robyn is terrified "What do they want?"

Gray shakes his head. "I don't know. Just go along with them until I can figure this out. We'll get out of this". But the sinking feeling in his gut is telling him otherwise and he silently curses himself for not getting Hopkins locked up when he had the chance.

CHAPTER 38

THE STORM

DECEMBER 25TH, 1974.

THE CAPTAIN OF THE BOOYA, a 36-metre, 262-ton, triple-mast freighter, turns her bow into the wind. He's weighed up his options and decided that his vessel has a better chance of survival out at sea. He pushes the engine to its full capacity and races towards the harbour entrance. The other five souls on board either cling on for dear life, or scurry about lashing down anything that could become a projectile. Each lightning strike reveals a new nightmare of green-tinged clouds, broiling seas and big, rolling waves.

The only female on board is twenty-four-year-old Ruth Vincent. Ruth works at a local bar and had met the Booya's captain on a few occasions. He'd told her there was nothing quite like seeing a storm from the ocean, and this storm was going to be unmissable. It was also obvious that he was as keen on her as she was on him. She'd promised her three children she'd be there when they woke on Christmas morning, but nights out, and adventures, are few and far between for a solo mum.

As the storm intensified, the captain told her to stay below deck for her own safety, but it was too claustrophobic, and she wanted to see what was happening, so she remained topside.

Off in the distance she can just make out another vessel – a ferry. "The Darwin Princess. Its captain also frequented the bar she works at.

The Booya crests wave after wave, each bigger than the last, as she valiantly cuts a path towards her goal. Another blinding lightning strike cuts across the sky, and the captain clocks the entrance to the harbour. It's no more than a half-click away, he calculates, confident that they'll make it.

The darkness descends on them again and in that moment a wind gust he guesses to be around 240 kilometres per hour hits into them like the shock wave from a massive bomb blast.

Ruth grabs the railing to stop herself from being hurled into the sea. She catches sight of the Darwin Princess capsizing, before a wave blocks her view. She screams in horror, but the wind snatches away the sound as it leaves her lips. A horrendous crack reaches her ears and she turns in time to see the stern mast fall, snapped at its base, still attached to the rigging. The heavy battering-ram arcs away from her as the vessel lists to port and she desperately clings to the starboard railing.

Ruth remembers a quote she shared with those closest to her: Live in hope, even if you die in despair. Now she feverishly clings to hope in the midst of despair. She wishes with all of her heart that she could be there in the morning to see her children's beautiful faces as they unwrap their Christmas presents. Her mind transports her there. Her children rush towards her, shouting, "Merry Christmas, Mum" The thought of it brings a smile to her lips. The mast swings back towards her with incredible momentum, ending that thought, and her life, in a heartbeat.

The shifting weight of the mast skews the Booya onto her starboard side and she's hit by a massive wave cresting over the top of her. The captain barely has time to lament his decision to try and outrun the storm before the vessel and all on board are sent to their deaths.

The wave hits with so much force that it drives her 22 metres to the bottom within seconds. The Booya slams into the seabed where she will remain, undiscovered, for the next twenty-nine years.

?

CHAPTER 39

"THIS IS INSANE, we've gotta head back to town" Wilks hears Johannson yell over the shrieking wind. The trees are bent under the power of the storm, and anything that isn't anchored down is whipped away into the bush.

"We can't just leave them out here. We have to wait," Wilks replies.

"You think they'd do the same for us?" Johannson counters.

This gives Wilks pause for thought.

"Nobody's going anywhere" he hears Hopkins call out.

Both men turn to discover Hopkins and Scotty herding Gray and Robyn into the campsite at rifle-point.

Wilks's brain goes into overdrive "What the bloody hell are you doing?" he screams at them.

At this point it becomes clear to Robyn that at least one of these men isn't in on the plan, and she pleads for reason. "You need to help us, before this goes any further" she desperately yells at Wilks.

Scotty pushes her hard and she stumbles to her knees. "Shut up, ya gin bitch" he says with a sneer.

Gray sees red and takes a swing at him, but Hopkins' rifle butt to his head stops him. He hits the mud beside Robyn, bleeding and semi-conscious. Fighting back the darkness, he rolls onto his back. "Listen to me" He tries unsuccessfully to focus on Hopkins. "This storm is a category four cyclone. We all need to leave – now. I swear to you, you let us go and we'll say nothing".

Johannson's thoughts are reeling "Are you out of your flamin' mind?" he screams at Hopkins and backs away as he strides towards him swinging the barrel of his rifle towards him.

Hopkins jabs the barrel of the rifle into Johannson's ample gut "In or out?" he growls.

Johannson can see in his eyes that Hopkins is well beyond reasoning with and is in no doubt that his life hangs on the next words out of his mouth. "Please, this is wrong" he whispers.

Hopkins drives the barrel deeper "You're either with us or you're against us".

"In" he whispers as he drops his gaze to the sodden ground.

Hopkins grabs him by the ear and wrenches him onto his toes getting a satisfying squeal of pain. "I can't hear you".

Johannson screams "In, in, flamin' in".

Hopkins releases Johannson's ear and turns to Wilks "In or out, Wilksy?".

Wilks, like Johannson, is in a whirlwind of confusion "Who the fuck are they?" he yells at Scotty.

Scotty punctuates his reply with a sharp kick into Gray's ribs "The smart arse Abo from the other night and his white Gin missus".

Wilks swipes the water from his eyes and slowly pieces it together "They're why we're out here?" The silence from Scotty and Hopkins is his answer.

Hopkins fronts up to Wilks and takes his face in both hands, forcing him to focus on his eyes "In or out?"

Wilks glances at the couple lying bleeding on the ground and back to Hopkins. He always knew that Hopkins was on the ragged edge, but now he can see that he has stepped into the abyss and it terrifies him "Nah, mate, this is too far. This is fuckin' crazy".

Hopkins doesn't blink as he squeezes Wilks's face harder between his hands "I like you, Wilksy, don't make me do something I might regret". He doesn't wait for an answer and turns to Scotty "Cover them".

Gray tries to plead one last time "I'm begging you, please, let Robyn go. She's done nothing to you. It's me you want".

Hopkins grabs Gray by the face with one hand and pulls him up as he glares into his eyes "You called the coppers and cost me my fuckin' job. All because of a little fun at your expense. You set this game in motion. Now you both get to play it out to the end". He retains his grip on Gray as he barks an order to Johannson "Fat fuck, grab a rope out of the dinghy".

Johannson hurries over to dinghy, grabs a length of rope, and returns, holding it out to Hopkins.

Hopkins doesn't take it "Dickhead" he spits and points to a tree at the river's edge with a branch hanging roughly four meters above the waters' surface "String the calf's head over that branch. Hang it a couple of feet off the surface".

If it was possible to go any paler, Johannson manages to do it "Uh, uh, not me, I'm not going out there" he mumbles as he backs away.

Hopkins pointedly swings the barrel of the rifle his way "Wilksy, give the fat fucker a hand. "You're both gonna get a kick out of this" he says to Gray as he pushes his face back into the mud.

Johannson and Wilks go to the dinghy, haul the calf's head out, and tie it to one end of the rope. Wilks helps a very scared Johannson scale the tree and passes the calf's head up to him "You'll be okay, just tie it off and come straight back".

Johannson nods nervously, balances the calf's head in one arm, shuffles along the branch on his arse cheeks. He stops above the water's edge, terrified. Hopkins voice reaches him from below "Further out!". Johannson looks back over his shoulder and yells "This is far enough". He begins to move the calf's head into place.

Hopkins chambers a round and fires it into the branch just behind his leg "Further out" he commands.

Johannson reluctantly shuffles forward until he reaches a point way out over the water and gets the nod from Hopkins "That'll do" before lowering the calf's head into position and tying it off. Johannson secures the last knot and turns to Hopkins "Are you bleedin' happy..?"

The bull crocodile explodes from beneath the water and locks onto the calf's head.

It thrashes and twists on the end of the rope while Johannson clings onto the branch for dear life. He screams as the branch bows and shakes under the immense weight of the croc.

Scotty takes a step back, caught of guard "Jesus, fuckin, Christ".

The rope snaps and the croc drags its prize beneath the surface.

Gray seizes the moment to scramble to his feet, punch Scotty in the face, and pull Robyn to her feet "Run" he yells and pushes her in the direction of the trees. She sprints towards the trees as fast as her legs will carry her.

Hopkins catches sight of Robyn hurtling towards the bush and snaps the rifle to his shoulder to bring her down.

"Mother fucker" screams Gray, as he charges Hopkins and barrels into him causing him to fire wide. Hopkins hits the ground with a bone crunching thud that knocks the breath out of him.

Gray regains his feet first and races toward the riverbank in an attempt to distract them giving Robyn more time to escape.

Hopkins rolls onto his knees, snaps the rifle up to his shoulder, and squeezes the trigger. It's a quick and poorly aimed shot, but the bullet still finds its target.

Gray is hit in the side of the head, spun off his feet, and lands in the river with an explosion of blood and water marking his entry.

Johannson climbs down from the tree and scans the river for any sign of Gray's body before turning to Hopkins in shock "What have you done?" he howls.

"What have we done, you fat fuck" Hopkins leaves him gaping, strides over to Scotty, and drags him to his feet "There's no going back now. Get her".

Scotty groggily retrieves his rifle and motions for Wilks to do the same "Come on" They lope off into the bush.

Hopkins watches them until they disappear from sight and then waves Johannson over to join him on the river bank "Come here, watch this". Johannson cautiously approaches and stays just out of reach.

Hopkins points out two glowing orbs cutting through the water "See that?" The bull crocodile cruises past, heading down river "Natures clean-up crew" he says in awe.

Johannson drops to his knees and projectile vomits onto the muddy ground, but Hopkins barely notices as he watches the powerful beast close-in on its prey. His thoughts take him back to a time when he was the apex predator.

CHAPTER 40

MAY 1ST, 1960, HACKNEY, UK.

THE MOLOTOV COCKTAIL EXPLODES ON IMPACT, instantly engulfing everything on the ground floor. The young Jamaican couple sleeping in the lounge wake to the sound of screaming, only to realize the screams are their own and they are burning alive. They shriek and writhe, searching for the exit, but the fire quickly overcomes them and they collapse to the floor.

Two men wearing balaclavas, trench coats and gloves are out in the street on either side of the house with three more deadly Molotov cocktails between them.

Two Jamaican men throw open the back door but never get to set foot outside. A Molotov cocktail is hurled at them and it slams into the doorframe. Liquid flames cover both men and they stagger blindly back into the burning house.

A young Jamaican woman, a baby swaddled protectively in her arms, appears at an upstairs window. The thick black smoke chokes her and her eyes stream with tears. She wrenches open the window and gulps in clean fresh air, before searching for a way down. Her eyes fall upon the man wearing the balaclava in the street. He holds his last Molotov cocktail up for her to see. She holds out her child silently, begging him to spare his life.

He lights the fuse and waits until the last possible moment. The girl tries to back away, but the flames behind her make retreat impossible. She realizes her life is over, but isn't prepared to let her child suffer the same fate.

He pitches the Molotov cocktail at the upstairs window and she tosses her baby into the garden below. The Molotov cocktail shatters the window and the girl is engulfed in burning fuel. He watches her thrash around the room like a Roman candle feeling zero remorse and peels up the balaclava so she can see what the face of vengeance looks like.

His uncle runs around the house and grabs Hopkins by the arm: "Cover your face, you bloody moron, unless you want to hang?".

His uncle turns to leave, but Hopkins is heading towards the burning house. "What the fuck are you doing?" he yells at him.

Hopkins points to the garden below the window. "She threw the baby out of the bloody window" he laughs. His uncle hurries over to him, and both of them gaze down at the baby. The fall has injured the infant, but he's still alive and crying.

His uncle grabs Hopkins by the sleeve "Leave it be, for fuck's sake. We're done" he orders.

Hopkins wrenches free of his grip. "Not yet" He raises his boot and crushes the infant's skull with a single savage blow silencing its cries forever.

"Oh, Sweet fucking Jesus," wheezes his uncle, and vomits through his balaclava.

The sound of police sirens fills the air, and frightened neighbours begin to emerge from their homes.

Hopkins pulls his balaclava down. "This is what we do" he says flatly. He drags his shaken uncle out of the yard, down the road, and through the shadows of familiar back alleys.
⍰

CHAPTER 41

GRAY BREAKS THE SURFACE, gasping for air. A blood trail leaches into the water around him. The crocodile locks onto him and picks up speed with a flick of its muscular tail. Gray sinks below the surface again and spots the crocodile heading straight for him. There's nothing he can do, no escape, but there is no fear. He reaches out his hand to touch the beast, just as he had in his dreams. At the last possible moment the crocodile pivots onto its side, jaws closed, and slides straight past him.

Gray pivots in the water and follows the crocodile as it moves away from him and disappears into the murky depths. He kicks for the surface, gulps in a huge lungful of air, and drains the last of his ebbing strength fighting the current to reach the far bank. He manages to pull himself halfway out of the river before his vision blurs and consciousness slips from him.

Strong brown hands grab him from above and haul him onto the bank. Lightning flashes across the sky, freezing the image of a mob of Indigenous rescuers standing above him. Gray is lifted between them and carried away from the river into the dense bush. In his delirious state he hears the shrieking wind, sees the trees bending before the storms mighty force, and is blinded by lightning streaking across the sky. He loses track of time and has no idea how far they have travelled.

They reach a steep rock face and carry him up to the safety of a cave.

Colours, sounds and images blend together in a kaleidoscope of memories coming at him with the speed and intensity of a strobe light. Gray floats somewhere between life and death, the physical world and the dreamtime.

Flash!

Gray slides through thick mud, knife in hand, the blade long and rusty. A wild boar cautiously approaches for a drink. Once it is preoccupied he darts forward and cuts its throat with a quick, brutal slash. He drags the boar into the water and slips below the surface.

Flash!

Lange gets out of his seat, walks stiffly towards the exit. His shoes strike the floor with an unnaturally loud boom. He disappears through the doors without as much as a backwards glance.

Flash!

A tribesman plays a haunting tune on a didgeridoo while two others dance. The story depicts a crocodile stalking its prey.

The tribesman pretending to be the crocodile swoops in close, arms snapping like the jaws of the beast.

Flash!

Gray crawls to the river's edge and stares at his reflection in the dark surface of the water. Everything around him is reflected, except for him. He holds out his hand and still no reflection. It's as though he doesn't exist in this realm.

Flash!

Lange collapse onto the floor and sawdust billows into the air.

Flash!

Lange's coffin slides into the crematorium's incinerator, the door closes, and it fills with flames.

Flash!

Lange towers above him, his mouth opens, but the voice is not his: "We don't own the land. The land owns us" says the old Indigenous man from the court room.

Flash!

A lightning strike lights up the cave walls. They are covered in Indigenous paintings depicting crocodiles, wild pigs, kangaroos, and Indigenous hunters. Ten Indigenous men and women sit around the walls of the cave.

Flash!

An Indigenous man, missing his front teeth, kneels and offers Gray water from a wooden bowl of water and watches as he drains it.

Flash!

The tribesman reaches out, touches Gray's chest, and runs his fingers over the smooth skin.
"Robyn?" Gray asks weakly.

Flash!

The toothless tribesman looks at the women and on cue they stand as one and exit the cave without a sound.

Flash!

The tribesman removes a knife from the dilly-bag hanging across his shoulder. Gray cries out, "No!" and tries to fight, but his muscles won't respond.

The other tribesmen watch from the shadows, their eyes piercing, all knowing. The tribesman slices the skin across Gray's chest in a series of V-shaped cuts.

Flash!

A scream cuts through the cave, echoing around the walls, but it isn't coming from Gray. The scream become a woman's screeching voice. The old Indigenous woman from the garden bar hovers horizontally above him. "Nowhere man," she hisses. "He's coming, Namarrkon is coming".

Lange is crouched beside him with his hand on his bloody chest. "Understand where you come from and the responsibility that bears." Lange holds out his blood-soaked palm for Gray to see. "Why are you so hell-bent on denying your truth?"

Flash!

Robyn is beside him. She puts her fingers to his lips. "We love you, we know who you are, and we need you to be strong".

Flash!

He is four years old again, and on the beach with his mother. She takes a knee in front of him. "We all face the storm one day" she says, gazing into his eyes.

She gently cradles his face in her trembling hands. "Face it and don't be afraid. I will be with you. Your people will be with you."

The words of his mother, words that had no meaning to the child, now mean everything to the man, and he fights to rise through the darkness enveloping him.

?

CHAPTER 42

BRANCHES TEAR AT ROBYN'S SKIN as she races headlong through the bush in a blind panic. The wind slows her pace, knocking her off balance, and the lashing rain reduces her visibility to a couple of metres at best. She trips on a log and goes down hard. Lightning streaks across the sky, turning the night to day for an instant.

"Where ya gonna go, love?" Scotty's calls out from the darkness.

Robyn quickly scrambles to her feet and scans the immediate area. He sounded close, but she sees nothing. Completely disoriented, she runs back the way she came.

Scotty calls out again: "There's nowhere to run out here".

She turns in the direction of his voice, loses her footing, and tumbles end over end to the bottom of an embankment. Dazed and bleeding, she drags herself into a sitting position. Her hand drops protectively over her belly as she feverishly looks around, trying to get her breath back and calm down.

Lightning crackles across the sky again, and Wilks is lit up standing in front of her.

Robyn quickly regains her feet, adrenaline fuelling her muscles. She spins and takes the first steps in the opposite direction, only to run straight into Scotty.

"Boo!"

She attempts to sidestep him, but he's ready for her, and grabs her by the throat. He slams her into the ground with enough force to drive the breath from her lungs and straddles her before she can regain her senses.

Robyn immediately begins thrashing, trying to dislodge him. "Get the fuck off me" she screams.

Scotty grins savagely. "That's no way for a lady to talk".

Wilks stands firm, but his eyes are lowered to the ground in shame.

Robyn quickly runs out of steam, exhausted with Scotty looking her over. Her wet clothes cling to her body, hiding nothing.

"Fuckin' nice" he grunts. His intent is obvious.

"Please don't, I'm pregnant" she pleads.

Her words and look of sheer desperation moves him and he has to try and help her. "Scotty, wait up" he says. "We can let her go. No one else has to get hurt".

"No one else has to get hurt" These words hit her like a punch in the gut. "What have you done to Gray?"

Scotty looks at her, a contemptuous smirk on his face, as he answers Wilks. "That ship sailed when we put a bullet in his fuckin' head".

Robyn's world crumbles. Gray, dead, her mind reels out of control.

Scotty roughly grabs her breasts and she doesn't react. "Not too fuckin' bad for a white gin". He pauses. "See'n as it's Christmas an' all, I've got you something". Still pinning her down, he undoes his pants with one hand and pulls out his erect cock. "It's a stockin' stuffer". He reaches for the zipper of her pants and is distracted as he fumbles to open it.

Her fingers curl around a tree branch. She screams, "Fuck you!" and hammers it into the side of his head, shoves him off her and painfully climbs to her feet. Robyn tries to run, but Wilks is blocking her path. She stares frantically into his eyes. "You know this is wrong" she yells at him.

His face is a mask of misery. "I'm sorry," is all he can manage, before Scotty looms up behind her, spins her around, and punches her in the face. She hits the ground hard and is barely conscious. He's on her in a flash with a knife held to her throat. "Now you're gonna bleed, bitch". He slices off her pants, rips her panties with his bare hands, and brutally drives into her. Blood mingles with rainwater and drips from his face onto hers.

A switch flicks in Robyn's mind and her world goes dark.
⁉

CHAPTER 43

GRAY OPENS HIS EYES and glances around, disoriented. There is a smouldering fire in the centre of the cave. He pushes himself into a seated position and leans back against the wall. The mob that pulled him from the river are huddled together against the opposite wall. The wind shrieking past the cave's entrance sounds like the turbines on a dozen Boeing 747s.

The Indigenous man who rescued him crosses the cave and squats beside him. "You lucky to be alive" he tells him. "That big croc, he spared you for something".

Gray has recollections of the crocodile passing by him and his saviours hauling him out. "That was you at the river?" he asks.

The man nods. "We were heading inland to get away from the storm, just bloody lucky we saw you".

Gray's thoughts snap back to Robyn. "How long has it been since you found me?" The image of Robyn out there alone, hunted and afraid, fills him with anguish. "How long?" he asks again.

"Maybe one hour" replies the man. He reaches out and touches the wound on Gray's head. "Them blokes that shot you, they still looking for you?"

He shakes his head. "They probably think I'm dead, but Robyn, my wife, she's still out there".

The man gazes into Gray's eyes. "If you gonna stop them blokes," he says with calm certainty. "You gotta become the storm. You know?".

Gray holds the man's eyes for a moment longer and whispers, "Namarrkon".

The Indigenous man nods his head, yes, and whispers the name back to him: "Namarrkon". The rest of the mob join in, and chant the name over and over. "Namarrkon," whisper the others, and they too point at him. The Indigenous man crosses his arms over his own chest. "Namarrkon," he says louder. He is holding something inside, or something is inside him, and then he points at Gray's chest: "Namarrkon".

It dawns on Gray that Namarrkon was never coming for him; the storm is brewing inside him, and now it's time for others to fear its fury.

The mob chant over and over: "Namarrkon", "Namarrkon", "Namarrkon". For the first time in his life, Gray feels a connection with something greater than himself. He crosses to the cave's entrance and, without hesitation, steps out into the shrieking wind.

?

CHAPTER 44

THE RENTAL FOUR-WHEEL-DRIVE SLAMS INTO THE
BANK, skews sideways in the air, and crashes into the
river. The engine continues to roar until its ports fill with
water and it dies. The current grabs the vehicle and it is
swept down river.

Hopkins and Johannson watch from a distance as the
vehicle disappears around the bend. "It'll look like they
lost control and crashed into the river" yells Hopkins.
"There'll be no trace of us ever being here when the
storm's done its job."

Johannson looks unconvinced, but keeps his mouth
shut. Lightning streaks across the sky, momentarily
freezing both men in its stark glare. "We'd better get
out of this shit". Hopkins staggers away with Johannson
following closely behind him.

Wilks is hauling sandbags onto the iron sheet roof when
Hopkins and Johannson arrive back at the camp, wind
tearing at their ponchos, and barely managing to stay
upright.

Hopkins grabs Wilks from behind and he jumps, startled:
"Bloody hell, give a bloke a heart attack, why don't ya?"

"Scotty and the woman?" Hopkins yells at Wilks, who
simply points inside.

Wilks pulls open the door and has to hold onto it or lose it to the wind. All three men enter and Hopkins pulls the door shut.

An oil lamp hanging from the roof dimly lights the interior. A set of buffalo horns adorns one wall; beneath them sits an old skillet-stove. A rusty children's bunk bed lines another wall, and a hammock is strung across the centre. The rifles are laid across a filthy makeshift wooden table.

Robyn, streaked with mud and blood, is huddled up in the corner on a filthy sleeping bag. There seems to be nothing going on behind her eyes.

Scotty grabs his crotch and leers at Hopkins. "She won't give you any trouble now".

Hopkins crouches in front of Robyn, waves his hand in front of her face, and gets no reaction. "You pair of cunts couldn't fuckin' wait, could you?"

"Don't fuckin' look at me," says Wilks. "I didn't lay a finger on her."

Scotty grins like the cat that ate the cream "I didn't use a finger either".

Hopkins glares at him. "Look at her". Robyn's gaze is fixated on the constant drips of water exploding onto her kneecap.

"We're not going anywhere in a hurry," says Wilks, trying to calm things down, "Who's up for a smoke?" He unpacks a tin from his backpack.

Johannson recognizes the box and moves to intercept it before Wilks can crack the lid, but Hopkins grabs him by the collar and drags him over to Robyn. "How about you, fat-fuck? You want some of this?"

Johannson replies, but his eyes remain fixated on what Wilks is doing. "Nah, I'll pass" he says, nervously.

Wilks is trying to pry the lid off the box but the oil makes it difficult.

Hopkins is puzzled. "You'll pass? When was the last time you fucked anything other than Mrs Palmer and her five daughters?"

Johannson is still looking at Wilks and Hopkins' anger flares. "What are you fucking looking at?" He grabs Johannson's face in one hand and forces him to make eye contact. "I asked you a question".

Johannson tries to keep it light, but inside he's shitting himself. "You know how it is," he says quietly.

"No, I don't know how it is," Hopkins replies.

"I don't want to go sloppy seconds" he feebly explains.

Scotty laughs. "Bullshit, you'd root the knothole in a tree if we put some fur around it".

The rain hammers into the roof and wind shrieks past the shed, but the sound of the box lid popping open is like a rifle shot to Johannson.

Wilks is confused as he looks at the boxes contents. "What the fuck?" Confusion quickly turns to disgust. He takes out a photograph of a naked young boy. He glares at Johannson. "She doesn't do it for ya, does she, ya fuckin' dirty prick?"

Johannson stares at him silently, his eyes pleading.

Hopkins looks from one to the other "What the fuck are you on about, Wilksy?"

Wilks flicks the Polaroid across the shed and it bounces off Johannson's head, landing face up on the floor.

Johannson scrambles for the photograph, but Hopkins beats him to it and looks at the image in disgust. White hot rage flares in Hopkins mind, and he explodes. He hits Johannson with a barrage of heavy punches, leaving him bruised and bloody.

Robyn stirs and her eyes focus on Hopkins towering above Johannson cringing on the floor.

"They're just photographs. I've never touched a child ..." he whines.

"Liar!" Wilks flicks another photograph and it lands face up on the table. In the picture, Johannson is buggering a young boy in his room and has taken this shot of them both reflected in the mirror.

Hopkins' blood freezes in his veins and his rage goes past the redline. "You've been in my fucking house!" He punctuates this with a boot to Johannson's ribs. The sound of bones cracking spurs him on.

Johannson screams in agony and raises his hands to ward off further blows.

"With my fucking kids" rages Hopkins, and boots him again, this time breaking his fingers with an audible snap. He grabs his rifle from the table and chambers a round.

"No!" screams Johannson.

"Hopkins!" yells Wilks.

"Don't, Wilksy, just fucking don't!" warns Hopkins.

"You can't just kill him" says Wilks.

But Hopkins' mind was made up the moment he saw that first image. "Do you want this paedo free to keep on doing this?"

Wilks takes a moment, and then slowly shakes his head, no.

Scotty throws in his two-cents-worth. "What's one fuckin' more, hey?"

Johannson wails at the verdict. "Please, I'm begging you. I'll get help. I will. I'm not well".

Scotty bursts out laughing. "A 303 capsule will take care of that. It's a guaranteed cure-all".

Hopkins takes aim at Johannson's head and slides his finger through the trigger guard, just as a wind gust hits the shed with a roar. A corner of the roof lifts off and the wind shrieks in. The oil-lamp falls to the floor, breaks, and a fire spreads quickly.

Hopkins yells to Scotty "Fuck's sake, get that."

Wilks and Scotty hurry to extinguish the fire with a grimy blanket.

Robyn seizes the opportunity, snatches a rifle from the table, and backs into a corner with the barrel panning across the men.

Hopkins swings the rifle away from Johannson and covers Robyn. "Drop it," he yells.

Johannson seizes the opportunity to escape, stumbles to his feet, crashes across the top of the table, and slams through the door.

Scotty makes a move to go after him, but Hopkins stops him without letting Robyn out of his sight. "Let him go" he yells.

"What the fuck?" Scotty replies.

"If the storm doesn't get him, we'll finish him tomorrow." The door slams repeatedly. "Secure the door before we lose it," Hopkins yells.

Scotty fights the strength of the wind, but finally manages to close it.

Hopkins smiles at Robyn, impressed with her balls. "Well, look at you. Now what, huh?"

Her eyes flit from one man to the other.

Hopkins lowers his rifle and motions for her to do the same. "You might get one of us" he says, "but then what do you think will happen?"

Robyn smiles grimly through her cracked, bleeding lips. "You'll be the one, you smug arsehole".

He calls her bluff and opens his arms wide to present a bigger target. "It takes a big set of balls to kill a..."

She squeezes the trigger before he can finish his sentence – click!

Hopkins' hand snaps out, wrenches the rifle from her grip, and spins it around. "You might wanna remember to take the safety off". He fires the rifle with the muzzle beside her ear, sending the bullet spiralling through the back wall. He reverses the rifle again and slams the stock into Robyn's face. Her forehead splits open under the blow and she drops unconscious the floor.

Wilks and Scotty finish dousing the flames. The roof is still flapping crazily, but no one moves. Hopkins throws Scotty the rifle. "Do what you want with her, then kill her and dump the body in the river with her old man". He turns to Wilks. "You and me are on the roof".

"She's pregnant" says Wilks. "Can't we just let her go?" he begs.

Hopkins grabs him by the scruff of the neck and pulls him face to face. "And then what? Spend the rest of our lives in a six by eight cage?"

Tears well in Wilks's eyes as he shakes his head, no.

"You're a good boy, Wilksy, but you've gotta leave the thinking to me". Hopkins releases him and leads him out into the storm, closing the door behind them.

Scotty drags Robyn up by her hair and the pain partially rouses her. "Two for fuckin' one." He punches her in the face, driving her back onto the edge of the bunk bed. He turns her onto her belly, drags his pants down and enters her anally. Robyn screams as the pain rips through her.

Wilks and Hopkins hear her scream over the shrieking wind. Hopkins hands the sandbag he's holding to Wilks and yells "Keep loading them on, but make sure you spread them evenly or it'll cave the roof in".

Wilks looks questioningly at him, where are you going?

Hopkins grins "Join us when you're done". He leaves Wilks and heads back inside the shed.

Wilks packs the sandbag onto the roof and Robyn's screams reach his ears over the storm.

He crouches down with his hands pressed tightly over his ears to block the sound out.

?

CHAPTER 45

"LORD, I SWEAR, YOU GET ME OUT OF THIS..."
Johannson prays. His heart feels like it's about to
explode and his lungs are on fire. He's probably put less
than a kilometre between him and that mad bastard,
Hopkins. He pulls up, out of breath, and surveys the
track ahead. The flood plain is up and the track is barely
distinguishable beneath the muddy waters. His track
markers are the trees and bushes lining either side. He
groans in pain, holding his injured arm tighter to his
broken ribs. With the pain comes fresh panic – What if
they're following me? He turns to scan the track behind
him and, as if on cue, a massive lightning strike turns
night to day.

Gray is standing in the middle of the track directly
behind him, dripping wet and shirtless. He has a solid
club-length branch in his hand and a hatred burning in
his eyes. The lightning disperses and Gray vanishes back
into the darkness.

Johannson peers into the night, but he can't see a damn
thing. "It's not me you want!" he screams into the pitch
black void, but the wind rips his words away as soon as
they leave his lips. "I couldn't give a shit if you kill that
bastard. You'd be doing the world a favour," he yells.

Gray attacks from the side of the track, hammering the
branch into Johannson's broken ribs.

Johannson screams and flails with his good arm, but Gray has already disappeared back into the bush.

Johannson turns towards town and sprints as fast as his legs will carry him. He glances over his shoulder, sees the track behind is clear and stops, totally exhausted. He forces himself to continue, and comes face to face with Gray once again. "I didn't touch your missus!" he screams, and staggers off the track and straight into the pig-wallow. He immediately sinks up to his waist in thick mud and water.

Gray stands silently at the edge of the wallow watching Johannson trying to pull himself out of the mud with his good arm and a tree root, but the root breaks away in his hand. He is wedged in and the water is slowly rising. Gray turns and heads back towards the river without so much as a word.

"You can't just leave me here to drown!" he begs. "I wanted to give you a chance. Come on".

Gray thinks about this for a moment and then throws him the branch. "See how long this'll keep you afloat". With that he turns and trots back towards the river.

Johannson's threats follows him into the darkness "You black bastard. I hope he guts you like a pig". After a moment, only the storm has a voice.
?

CHAPTER 46

A HAND CLAMPS ONTO WILKS' SHOULDER and he spins around with his fists held up defensively. The pelting rain blurs his vision and he quickly wipes his eyes to clear them. Hopkins towers above him. "I could have cut your throat, Wilksy. You can't afford to be asleep at the wheel." At this stage Wilks couldn't give a shit about anything Hopkins has to say. He's spent the last half an hour working up the courage to tell him he's done and he's taking the woman with him.

Before Wilks can say anything, a huge streak of lightning splits the sky and Gray is lit up for all to see at the riverbank. "Jesus" Wilks is so stunned that he stumbles backward over his own feet and crashes into the side of the shed.

Hopkins follows his line of sight and gets a glimpse of Gray with his arm drawn back, before darkness descends once more.

Hopkins is in disbelief "I killed you. You're dead!" he yells. A barrage of rocks thrown in quick succession hits him and Wilks with enough force to draw blood. Hopkins unslings his rifle and fires randomly in the direction the rocks are coming from.

Bullets snap past the tree Gray is taking cover behind. The instant the shooting stops he races deeper into the bush.

"Things just got interesting" Hopkins drops his head, fighting the wind, and staggers into the bush, Wilks following closely behind.

"Interesting?" Wilks mutters to himself and follows him.

They reach the treeline and Hopkins signals to Wilks to spread out. They move deeper into the bush and further down river as the storm intensifies around them.

Hopkins stops beside a fallen tree and signals to Wilks: Can you see him? Wilks signals back: Nothing. They continue moving deeper into the bush and further away from the shed.

The mud beneath the fallen tree swirls and sucks as Gray pries his body from its grip and rises to his feet. He make certain that Hopkins and Wilks are still heading away from him before picking up a long branch, testing its strength, and lopes back towards the shed.
?

CHAPTER 47

ROBYN LIES NAKED AND BLEEDING on the bunk, almost catatonic, and curled into a foetal position.

Scotty backs away from her. "It's been fun" he says, pulling up his jeans and zipping his fly. He grabs her by the ankles and wrenches her towards him. "But all good things must come to an end". The door is ripped open behind him. "Do you cunts live in a fuckin' barn?" he yells, turning towards the door.

Gray fills the doorway, the jagged branch in his hands levelled at Scotty's chest. The sound of the door crashing repeatedly into the shed wall, and the shrieking wind add to the unfolding nightmare.

Scotty looks like he's seen a ghost. "Oh, fuck off" he whispers, and then laughs at how absurd this seems to him.

Gray clocks Robyn lying on the floor. Seeing what they've done to her pushes him over the edge.

"Yeah, sorry about that" sneers Scotty, as he lunges for his rifle.

A primal roar rises from deep in Gray's gut. He charges Scotty, driving the branch into his chest before he can get to the rifle.

Gray forces him back against the table and it collapses under their combined weight. Scotty is pushed further back until the bunk bed against his back stops him. His slick, bloody hands grasp the branch, trying to stop it penetrating deeper into his chest, but Gray relentlessly pushes forward. Scotty's breast bone and ribs snap, his throat fill with blood and it spews from his mouth. His head lolls back and the lights go out for good.

The door gives up the fight as the wind rips it from its hinges and hurls it skyward. It's enough to spur Gray back into action. He kneels in front of Robyn. "Rob, it's me" She doesn't respond and he's acutely aware that they're vulnerable unless they move quickly. He clocks her torn, saturated, clothes on the floor and tears the blanket from the bed. He cuts a hole in the centre with Scotty's knife and drapes the makeshift poncho over her head, and then looks for something to tie around her waist, Scotty's belt. He tries not to look at Scotty's eyes as he removes his belt, and then fastens it around Robyn's waist. He grabs both rifles from amongst the wreckage of the table, slings them across his back, and gently pulls Robyn to her feet. "Rob, we have to go." He drapes her arm over his shoulder; his goes around her waist, and he guides her out into the storm.

?

CHAPTER 48

JOHANNSON CHOKES ON A MOUTHFUL OF MUDDY WATER and violently coughs it up. The wallow is as deep as it's going to get and the excess has breached the crest. He's tired and struggling to stay upright with only the stick Gray threw him for support. He spits muddy water and takes a deep breath. Stay calm, he silently tells himself. The storm will blow itself out eventually, the water will recede, and you will walk out of here – No, run out of here.

The edge of the wallow acts like the wall of a dam. A section of it has broken away under the volume of the water and this is allowing excess water to run off. What if the break were bigger? he thinks. Bigger break equals more runoff. It's a slim chance, but it's the only one he's got. He takes his weight off the stick and reaches out with it. Bone grates against bone as his ribcage and cartilage stretch. "Fuck!" he screams, almost blacking out as white-hot pain shoots through his body. He shakes his head to clear it. "You faint, you die" he tells himself.

Slowly, gingerly, he extends the stick again. It's an agonizing stretch, but he manages to reach the edge with the tip. Very slowly, with laser focus, he begins to widen the break.

A powerful gust of wind snaps a tree beside the wallow at its base and slams it into the ground close to him. Johannson loses his balance and disappears below the surface. He claws at the bottom to right himself, but his hands just sink in the mud. He flails his good arm and his hand comes into contact with the stick bobbing on the surface. He drives it into the mud, pushes himself upright, breaches the surfaces, and desperately sucks in much-needed air. As soon as his nerves settle he pushes through the pain barrier, reaches out with the stick again, and continues digging.

?

CHAPTER 49

"I'M GONNA TEAR HIS FUCKING BLACK HEART OUT" swears Hopkins as he pulls the branch from Scotty's chest and tosses it aside.

Wilks can't watch, so he turns his attention to searching the shed for Scotty's and Johannson's rifles, finding neither. "He's got the other rifles," he says to Hopkins in a mild panic.

Hopkins finds his pack and pulls out a box of cartridges. "Nothing's changed" he says, as he reloads his rifle and pockets the rest of the cartridges. "I swear, mate. That bastard's gonna pay. I swear it". His eyes brim with tears and he angrily wipes them away. "Reload and let's go". He doesn't wait for an answer and heads outside.

Wilks digs out a box of cartridges from his pack and crouches in front of Scotty's corpse. "In the end, we all get what's coming to us," he whispers into his ear.

"Wilksy!" Hopkins bellows from outside.

Wilks loads a cartridge into his rifle and exits the shed into the driving rain.

He fights the wind to join Hopkins, who is using the Toyota as cover. "Why didn't he just take the four-by?" he yells to Hopkins.

Hopkins digs into his pocket and pulls out the keys. "You think I'd be stupid enough to leave the keys in the ignition?"

A gust of wind hammers through the campsite with incredible force. Both men are knocked off their feet and sent tumbling into the bush. Hopkins loses his grip on the keys and they land in the mud beside the campfire.

The Toyota is hit broadside and shunted a few feet sideways. A stronger gust follows and the shed is literally torn apart. Sheets of corrugated iron spin up into the air; the entire contents of the shed go with them, including Scotty's corpse, which disappears into the pitch-black night.

A sheet of corrugated iron slices through the air like a guillotine and slams into the tree just above their heads. The wind gust is over almost as suddenly as it began, and only the slab remains where the shed once stood.

Hopkins scrambles to his feet and scans the sky. "Fly, you little fuck!" he yells into the darkness. "Fly!" He draws back the rifle's bolt to make sure it's clear, checks, and once satisfied that it is, slides the bolt home. He turns to Wilks and grins. "Let's finish this". He leaves the cover of the trees, leans into the wind. "Come on!" and heads inland.

Wilks weighs up his options: turn around and hike out alone or stick with Hopkins. The urge to turn and run is strong, but now there's no doubt in his mind that Hopkins would find him and put a bullet in his head. He struggles against the wind and follows the mad bastard into the bush.

[?]

CHAPTER 50

GRAY HAULS ROBYN UP THE STEEP ROCK FACE towards the cave entrance, twenty or so metres above. The rain and wind pound them, and lethal debris slices through the air. He leads her into the cave and the waiting arms of the mob still who are taking shelter within.

The Indigenous women help Robyn to sit beside the fire and hug her between them, sharing body heat. Gray crouches in front of her and takes her face in his hands. "I'll lead them away and go for help." His words literally fall on deaf ears as she stares vacantly past him. "They can't hurt you anymore," he promises. "You're with friends."

Robyn's hands slowly drop to her crotch, and when she pulls them back they are covered in blood. A low moan escapes her lips and her body rocks back and forth.

One of the Indigenous women lifts the poncho and takes a look. She turns a tearful eye to Gray. "She lost that baby, proper."

All of the Indigenous women take this on as though it were their child, shed tears of grief, and wail to the heavens above.

Tears of pure savage rage fill Gray's eyes, spilling down his cheeks.

He stumbles backward, as though physically hit. "Dead, they're dead, all of them" he hisses furiously.

He unslings one of the rifles and hands it to the man who pulled him from the river. "Keep her safe" he orders.

The man takes the rifle and nods his head. "Them white fellas won't get past us".

Gray strides out of the cave and is quickly swallowed up in the raging storm.

Robyn sways back and forward, moaning softly. She picks up a rock and hits herself on the forehead with it. Blood seeps from the wound at her hairline. She strikes again and again. Her mind is operating on a deeper, primal, instinct. The other women join her. Together they externalize the pain, drawing it from within, and forcing it out.

?

CHAPTER 51

THE CREATURE LUNGES FOR WILKS and he fires a round at it. Lightning rips across the sky and he gets a stark look at the second anthill he's shot in the last couple of minutes. He's not sure how long it's been since he and Hopkins became separated, but minutes seem like hours. The gale-force wind-gusts and driving rain have turned him around and he has no idea where he's going.

Another streak of lightning shoots across the sky, lighting up the night and bringing the anthills to life. Wilks clocks movement to his right and swings the rifle around, but before he can fire - Hopkins appears out of the deluge and snatches the rifle from his hands.

"For fuck's sake" he yells. "That last shot nearly took my fucking head off". He checks the chamber of Wilks' rifle, and then hands it back to him. "I thought it was the Abo. I almost fucking shot you".

Wilks opens his mouth to explain how scared he is, how confused he feels, but tears beat the words and his body shudders with the force of the emotions ripping him apart.

"Don't lose your shit on me, Wilksy" yells Hopkins. "We need to stick together or we're dead. You got it?"

Wilks wipes the tears from his eyes. "I thought I saw someone, something..."

"Don't think, know" yells Hopkins, and he leads him over to the tallest and thickest of the anthills, where they get a break from the wind and can rest up for a minute. Hopkins checks his watch. "Just gone six and still darker than a coon's arsehole. All this cloud cover's not helping either. We'll wait here until sun up".

Wilks ejects the spent cartridge from the chamber and hesitates before removing the mag from the rifle. "I'm done, mate" he says, handing the rifle to Hopkins.

"That bastard killed Scotty, and you're just gonna let it fuckin' slide?" Hopkins yells as he balls his hand into a fist.

"After what we did to him and his missus..." says Wilks.

Hopkins is fast reaching boiling point. "You don't just get to walk away, Wilksy".

Wilks looks Hopkins dead in the eyes and makes his stand. "Then you're gonna have to shoot me, cause I'm fuckin'..."

The projectile punches through Wilks' leg just above the knee, tearing through ligament and muscle and leaving a gaping exit wound.

The rifle report follows a thousandth of a second later. Wilks collapses to the sodden earth, clutching his wounded leg, and screaming in agony. "Jesus! I've been shot. I've been fuckin' shot!".

Hopkins drops to the ground beside him. "The next one will be through your thick head if you don't shut up and start looking for something to shoot back at". He hands him back his rifle and unbuckles Wilks' belt. He shuffles around on his belly and straps the belt above the bullet entry point. Wilks screams as Hopkins tightens the strap. "Suck it up" snarls Hopkins.

The early morning light shows faintly through the cloud cover, but the rain and wind continue unabated. Wilks scans the treeline. "Jesus, it fuckin' hurts" he moans.

Water runs into Hopkins' eyes, blurring his vision. He wipes it away "We can't stay here. All he has to do is flank us and he'll pick us off one at a time".

Wilks states the obvious: "I don't think I can walk".

"Then lay down covering fire for me" says Hopkins.

Wilks nods his head, okay.

Hopkins checks the chamber. "I'll get to the treeline, come up behind him, and put a bullet in his thick skull" He scrambles to his feet and races for the treeline.

Wilks randomly fires round after round at the trees. Click! The hammer falls on an empty chamber. He tosses aside the rifle and closes his eyes, praying for an end to the madness he's become trapped in "I'm sorry, Mum" he mumbles before falling into semiconsciousness. For a brief moment there's total blackness – no sound, nothing, just sweet oblivion. Slowly, the sound of the driving rain and shrieking wind penetrates his subconscious and drags him back to reality. Wilks opens his eyes and discovers Gray standing directly in front of him, dripping wet, with the business end of a rifle aimed at his head.

"I guess me mum was right" he says in resignation and leans his forehead against the muzzle. "Gonna die stupid" He closes his eyes and accepts his fate as Gray's finger slowly squeezes the trigger.

Hopkins carefully moves through the bush; every step is calculated. The sound of a single rifle report coming from the direction he'd left Wilks stops him in his tracks. "Wilksy" he whispers to himself "Fuck". He starts walking again, slowly picking up speed, until he's running towards the river.

⏑

CHAPTER 52

THE RIFLE SHOT echoes around the cave as Robyn, blood dripping down her face, stumbles out of the entrance. She stands, buffeted by the howling wind, at the edge with the long, inviting, drop to the rocks below.

The tribesman is close, watching her from the mouth of the cave.

Robyn slowly leans forward, but the strong hand of the tribesman on her shoulder prevents her from falling. She looks back into his eyes and sees her own reflection mirrored in the deep brown of his pupils. It's a moment that feels like an eternity.

CHAPTER 53

THE MUD SUCKS HIM DEEPER and Johannson's mouth fills with water. In desperation, he thrusts the stick harder and harder against the embankment. The stick wedges in the clay and he loses his grip on it. Not only has he lost his digging tool, but it's now acting like a plug and the water begins to rise again. He slips deeper into the mud and his nose is now under water too. His eyes bulge as panic overwhelms him. Dear God, not like this, his mind screams, anything but this.

It seems that God answers him, as a section of the wallow gives way and the stick is carried through with the flow. The force of it breaks away more clay and Johannson is able to breathe as the water recedes.

The hammering rain stops as quickly as it started. He laughs quietly and it builds into a joyous hysteria that pierces the sudden stillness.

CHAPTER 54

THE STORM

GEOFF CRANE AND GARY HOLLAND crawl out from beneath their desk on the eight floor of the Bureau of Meteorology. The windows are shattered, the ceiling and electrical conduits are hanging down, and the floor is saturated.

Gary's mind is still reeling from the non-stop onslaught and lack of sleep. His shift finished at eleven last night, but the storm had made it too dangerous to drive home.

His mate Mick was on vacation, staying with him, Christine, and little Gary. A few days ago they'd put in place precautions, just in case Tracy hit them hard. Food, water, torches, and essentials were part of that, but strapping his four-wheel-drive under the house was the big one. It had a solid external roll cage and he'd jammed it where it would make it a compact, safe cocoon.

Gary had spent the night fluctuating between faith and flat-out despair, praying his family and Mick had made it into the vehicle. He slouches over to the window, unconsciously picking up sodden paperwork from the floor, and gazes out over the suburbs gasping in shock. "Oh my god!"

The destruction of the city is overwhelming. Almost every house has been ripped apart and debris is strewn everywhere. The airport terminal is still standing, but the aircraft have been flipped onto their backs or slammed into buildings. More and more images come at him, one after the other, until sensory overload fills his heart with grief and his eyes with tears. "Our Father, who art in heaven, hallowed be thy name ..." he prays. "... Give us this day our daily bread, and ..." The tears turn into sobs and he can't finish the prayer.

Geoff joins him at the window and holds him until the tears abate. "I have to get home. Christine, Gary ..." A sob cuts off his words. "They'll be fine. I know they're fine. Mick knew what to do" he reassures himself.

Geoff pulls his car keys from his pocket. "I'll drive you, if my car's still in one piece". They pick their way through the glass, upturned furniture, force open the stairwell door, and make their way down the eight floors to street level.

⍰

CHAPTER 55

HOPKIN BURSTS INTO THE CLEARING and makes a beeline for his vehicle. He digs into his pocket for the keys and comes up empty handed. "Fuck." He searches his memory and remembers dropping them earlier. He scans the ground, but can't see them anywhere. The river – he can take the dinghy and go up river, sink it, and then disappear.

The dinghy's on its side, but it still looks structurally sound. Hopkins grabs the edge of the hull and grunts under the weight as he lifts. A bullet slams into the engine cowling, and Hopkins dives for cover behind the dinghy. He scans the immediate area, nothing, save the flowing water, unnaturally loud in the vacuum created by the silence.

"What does it feel like, Hopkins, to be the hunted?" calls a voice. Gray is concealed behind that crop of ironbark trees.

Hopkins targets his voice and fires in that direction, hitting nothing. "Where are you, you black bastard?" he yells, enraged by the gnawing feeling taking hold in his gut – fear.

"It's you, Hopkins" He hears Gray, loud and clear. "You have no land to call your own, no soul to ground you. You're the one who's lost. You're the Nowhere man".

Hopkins pinpoints where he thinks Gray's voice is coming from, rolls onto one knee, and takes steady aim. "Come on, stick your head up" he says quietly to himself. "How's that pretty wife of yours?" he yells. "We fucked her six ways to Sunday and she loved it".

Gray refuses to be baited into making a fatal mistake and swallows the rage, for now.

Hopkins fires a round into the fallen tree he suspects Gray is hiding behind, and quickly chambers another.

The sound of whispering Indigenous voices comes from everywhere and nowhere all at once. "Nowhere man, Nowhere man, Nowhere man," over and over again. Hopkins frantically scans the surrounding area. A hole is punched into the hull of the dinghy centimetres from his head and the report follows an instant later.

Hopkins fires at a fallen tree again and reloads as he charges towards it. He jumps onto the tree trunk and fires, but Gray has already gone and the rifle is lying discarded in the dirt. Hopkins checks the magazine and chamber, finds both empty. He scans the ground for signs of the direction Gray has taken. "You know you did me a favour, taking out the others".

There are slide marks across the muddy riverbank, with hand prints on either side. He cautiously heads towards the river.

"Wilksy was a good cunt, but the soft cock would have broken the moment they sat him down in an interview room". Hopkins struggles through the mud sucking at his boots, and wades into the water. He can see the big bull crocodile on the bank further upstream, and keeps one eye on him. "And Johannson, I hope you fucked that paedo up, but it doesn't matter. He couldn't have gone far". He pushes through chest-deep water to reach the far bank. "There'll only be one story about what happened out here, and that'll be mine". The current created by the storm isn't as strong anymore, but Hopkins still has to fight to keep his balance and this takes a lot of his focus.

Gray rises from the water behind him, knife in hand, knocks the rifle aside with one hand and holds the knife to Hopkins' throat with the other. Hopkins has no choice but to drop the rifle into the river and wrap both hands around Gray's knife hand. For a brief moment they are locked together like macabre lovers. Hopkins twists Gray's wrist against the joint, causing him to lose his grip on the knife. It falls into the river and sinks straight to the bottom. Hopkins launches a frenzied attack, pummelling Gray with blow after blow, knocking him senseless, and driving his head beneath the rivers surface. Gray thrashes around and quickly runs out of air.

The big bull crocodile stirs. Its eyes snap open, alert. He lumbers to his feet, slips quietly into the murky water, and effortlessly glides towards the two men.

Gray ceases to fight and Hopkins loosens his grip on him. Gray plants his feet and fires an uppercut into Hopkins' jaw that lifts him off his feet. He dives onto Hopkins and holds his head beneath the surface. Hopkins thrashes wildly for a moment before going limp. Gray waits a little longer before dragging him, coughing and wheezing, to the surface.

Hopkins is defiant in the face of defeat. "You fucking black cunt". He punctuates the insult by spitting a wad of phlegm into Gray's face "Finish it".

Gray pushes Hopkins backward into deeper water. "You're not worth it".

Hopkins glares at him with burning hatred. "Fuckin' gutless" he sneers, as he floats away and sinks below the surface.

Gray scans the water's surface, but Hopkins doesn't reappear and frankly, he couldn't give a shit. He wades towards the bank, and discovers the tribesmen and women from the cave watching him from the shore. He's exhausted, but still manages to raise a hand in greeting.

The tribesman who pulled him from the river urgently points behind him, his eyes widening in alarm. Gray flicks a look back and sees Hopkins rise out of the water, his rifle cocked, locked, loaded, and aimed directly at him. It's all happening so quickly and there's nothing he can do.

Hopkins squeezes the trigger, but the rifle never gets to bark. A bullet tears into his chest, drives him off his feet, and hurls him back into the river.

Gray looks for the shooter and discovers Robyn in the centre of the mob, blood streaked across her determined face, the smoking rifle still aimed at Hopkins. "I didn't forget the safety this time" she whispers.

Hopkins struggles to regain his feet and brings the rifle to bear on Robyn, lines her up in the sights, and slips his finger over the trigger. "Fucking bitch". He clocks Gray screaming a warning: "Robyn!" and racing to put himself in the line of fire. Hopkins aim steadies and he squeezes the trigger.

The big bull crocodile explodes from the water. Its powerful jaws slam shut around Hopkins' torso and drive him beneath the surface.

He screams, an explosion of bubbles, as the crocodile takes him down and twists him in a savage death-roll, snapping his spine. Hopkins immediately loses all motor function, but he's still very much alive.

The crocodile surfaces and carries him up river in its jaws. Hopkins has hunted enough crocs to know that he'll be stuffed under a log until his body rots and then pulled apart. He's never been a religious man, but he's praying to God to end his life right fucking now – God isn't listening.

Gray trudges through the mud and onto the riverbank. He gently removes the rifle from Robyn's shaking hands and she throws herself into his arms. He holds her to his chest "You did good, Rob". He hands the rifle to the nearest tribesman. "Thank you" he says, and then helps Robyn back to the Toyota, the mob follow them every step of the way. The women circle and embrace Robyn, and she them, before being helped into the passenger seat.

Gray hurries around to the driver's side and discovers the keys are missing. "Shit. No key". A quick scan of the shed's foundation and the clearing by many eyes reveals the keys lying in the mud beside the campfire. Gray scoops them up and says his goodbyes to the rest of mob ending on his saviour. "I don't know how I can ever thank you".

The man takes his hand. "You remember the people, the land, where you belong" he says "And one day, you come back".

"I will, I promise" replies Gray, and shakes his hand before climbing into the drivers side. After several attempts to start the Toyota, it finally splutters into life. They slowly drive away and catch a last glimpse of the mob in the rear-view mirror as they take ownership of their new dinghy and rifles.

Robyn gazes out of the window at the passing bushland as Gray concentrates on keeping them on the track. The storm has passed but the landscape is still below water. Tears well in her eyes and she angrily wipes them away. "They don't get one tear from me. Not one". She leans into him, seeking his warmth.

He drops an arm across her shoulders and holds her tightly "I love you, Rob" he whispers as tears well in his eyes and spill down his cheeks. So strong is his love for her that he sheds the tears she won't.

[?]

CHAPTER 56

WILKS HOBBLES FROM HIS HIDING PLACE on a makeshift crutch fashioned from a twisted, gnarly, branch. His knee is crudely splinted with sticks and his belt. He'd heard the Toyota coming and fearing it was Hopkins, hid off to the side of the track. He had watched from cover as the vehicle passed with Gray at the wheel and Robyn beside him.

His thoughts go back to the moment he had leaned his forehead against the muzzle of Gray's rifle "I guess me mum was right. Gonna die stupid" Wilks had uttered what were essentially going to be his last words in this life.

Gray had squeezed the trigger, but couldn't bring himself to finish it. He'd pointed the rifle skyward. "Start walking, and turn yourself in. If you come back I will kill you" He'd squeezed the trigger and fired a round at the clouds.

Wilks slowly shuffles along the track on his makeshift crutch. Each step is agony and the crutch keeps sinking in the mud, but at least he's alive, and for that he is grateful. He can hear the grunting and squealing before he sees the drift. Not far ahead is the muddy wallow, and it's swarming with wild pigs. The more wary scatter as Wilks approaches, but not the big boar, who defiantly stands his ground.

Wilks wants to get by, but the boar is a serious threat. "Go on! Get out of it!" he yells, with more bravado than he actually feels.

The boar stands him off for a moment longer before trotting away, revealing Johannson's partially consumed body still trapped in the mud. Flaps of torn flesh hang in tatters from his face, shoulders and chest, and he's been eviscerated. Drowning would have been a blessing – Be careful what you wish for.

Wilks stares at the corpse for a long moment "Bush bloody justice" he finally says, before hobbling along the track towards town.

CHAPTER 57

THE STORM

GEOFF CRANE AND GARY HOLLAND stand beneath the remains of Gary's house. Like all of those surrounding it, his has been shaved off its foundations, leaving only the floor and the concrete stilts. Gary's four-wheel-drive is still strapped under the house and his family is safe because of it.

Gary's wife, Christine, and his mate, Mick, are searching through the remains on the first floor, looking for clothing and anything else that might help them over the coming days. It's tough going and the pickings are slim.

Geoff and Gary watch his son, Gary junior, pick through the debris littering the front lawn. He finds a fake Christmas tree under a piece corrugated roofing iron. It's a bit of a struggle for the youngster but he's determined. He finally wrenches the tree out and spends the next few minutes straightening out the twisted wire branches. Once he's satisfied with his work he takes the tree to the end of the driveway and stands it up for all to see. He turns back towards Geoff and Gary with a huge, gap-toothed smile on his face. "Merry Christmas, Daddy. Merry Christmas, uncle Mick, and mummy too" he calls out.

The tears both men shed over his words confuses him and his smile falters. Seeing this, Gary hurries over to his son, sweeps him up in his arms, and kisses his face over and over again. "Merry Christmas" he says to him, as he looks down at this symbol of hope created by the hands of his child. "Merry Christmas" he repeats.

Christine and uncle Mick join them on the driveway and the four of them cling together in front of the Christmas tree.

EPILOGUE

MELBOURNE, VICTORIA, NOVEMBER, 1976.

MOTHS DANCE AROUND THE BARE LIGHT BULB hanging from the rafters of Lange's garage. Gray's face is a study of concentration as he taps away with a fine chisel and a craft hammer. He puts the tools aside and gently brushes away the last of the wood shavings from his work. His dreamtime crocodile is carved into the wood for all time, and below it are the words: Your journey is our journey.

Gray switches off the light and closes the door behind him as he leaves the garage. Moonlight streams through the window, highlighting the crocodile and the mantra.

Gray wanders through the kitchen where he shared many a meal and conversation with Lange. He tiptoes through the lounge, past the family photographs, and pauses for a moment to reflect on his memories. He's glad they decided to sell their place and move into Lange's. As yet they've made no changes, just happy to surround themselves in the healing cloak of the past. It's been a slow process, but they are getting there, and are acutely aware they will have to live with it for the rest of their lives, but both of them are determined not to let it control their future.

Gray checks the clock on the wall – only six hours before he's due in court. His previous employer had been disgruntled, to say the least, when he told them he'd be representing his people in their struggle to regain their land rights. Old colleagues stopped speaking to him, and some would rather cross the street than say hello. None of this really bothered him, in fact, it made him more resolute – He has been awakened.

He picks up a framed photograph of Lange "Good night, old man, I love you" he whispers, before putting it back and turning out the lights.

Gray quietly enters the master bedroom, guided only by a slither of light peeking through the curtains. He undresses and slips under the covers with Robyn.

She moans softly and her body rocks gently from side to side. The nightmares were brutal for her at first, but slowly, over the past couple of years, her sleep had become deeper, more peaceful. Counselling, her art, and his support, had gradually brought her back from the darkest of days.

He presses his chest against her back and the moment their bodies connect she calms and the rocking slowly ceases. He gently slides his hand across her waist and cradles her swollen belly.

The size of the bump reminds him that the baby is due in less than a month – a boy, he secretly prays. Baby Lange, born on or close to Christmas Day.

As Gray's eyelids droop and sleep begins to take him, he thinks of Hopkins as he sometimes does. He could never openly articulate this to anyone, and he doubts they would understand anyway. His growth, his spiritual awakening came, in part, from that brutal experience. The act of birth and rebirth are filled with pain. With that final thought, he drifts into a deep peaceful sleep, with his family safe and secure in his arms and a future full of infinite possibilities.

THE END

FOR MARTY WILKS 1961 ~ 2022

Printed in Great Britain
by Amazon

84563756R00119